RIVER
WEATHER

RIVER WEATHER

STORIES

CAMERON MACKENZIE

Alternating Current Press
Boulder, Colorado

River Weather
Cameron MacKenzie
©2021 Alternating Current Press

Alternating Current
Boulder, Colorado
press.alternatingcurrentarts.com

ISBN: 978-1-946580-29-0
First Edition: December 2021

TABLE OF
CONTENTS

For Frank

Having gone so high as we could with the bote, we met Savages in Conowes ... and places where the waters had falne from the high mountains had left a tinctured spangled skurfe that made many bare places seeme as guilded.

—Captain John Smith,
Generall Historie of Virginia, 1624

RIVER WEATHER

SCENARIOS

When I was in seventh grade or thereabouts, I had a suicide scenario, the particulars of it representative of the age and time. My plan was, so I would tell friends after school by the bike path, to strap a large speaker to my chest connected to a Walkman in my pocket, and jump out of a plane. On the way down as I tore through the clouds, I'd play "Fade to Black" from Metallica's *Ride the Lightning* album.

My plan generally earned appreciative nods from all around and would kick off interesting debates, such as whether "Fade to Black," with its subdued opening and almost seven-minute run time, was really the best song to play when jumping out of a plane to one's death. Point taken. We decided I'd have to start the song about three minutes and fifteen seconds in to reach maximum intensity before impact.

The other principal objection concerned the impact itself. Wouldn't it be better, my friend Jerry suggested, to shoot yourself in the head before you hit the ground? While some argued that the pain associated with either situation would be negligible, we did find some aesthetic appeal in holding a revolver for this final wingless flight into the unknown. Whether I would've gotten the pistol to my head in time, or whether I would've even chosen to use it after everything else, remains an unanswered question.

And then there was the possibility, put forward by always conscientious Scott, aspiring physicist Scott, that I might not be able to hear Metallica properly at that altitude and speed, what with the wind in my ears and the behavior of soundwaves.

Jerry objected. "The song's not for him," he said. "It's for the people on the ground."

I hadn't considered this but immediately adopted it, nodding sagely, and smiling at those in the circle who'd gathered around to listen.

KALIM MANSOUR

"You have to know what they are," my father told me as I turned his car onto the road. "You have to know what they're like. Because ask yourself this. Ask yourself who signs up to be a cop. Ask yourself who wants to bully his own people. You want to be a hero? Go be a Marine, get your ass shipped off to who knows where. You want to serve your community? Go put out fires. No. Cops like power, and they like control. And you've got to let them feel like they've got it, regardless of what they really are. Because they do."

"Do what?"

"*Jesus* son," my father hissed. "Listen: you do exactly what a cop says when they say it, and you do it with a smile. Don't look at me like that, I'm giving you the truth."

My father sat in the passenger seat of his brand

new Acura Legend, his eyes flicking up and back the empty nighttime roads as I made a right on red. It was my first time driving my father's new car, stacked as it was with floor-to-ceiling leather and wood paneling and softly glowing dashboard lights. Having just turned 15, it was one of the first times I had driven a car at all. This was Christmas break, and the main drag of my grandmother's two-stoplight town was black and silent, the roads dusted at the edges with salt.

The car, I had decided, was beautiful—both elegant and powerful in a way that surpassed my father. The car seemed beyond him even as it raised him in my estimation and affected my understanding that he was, in fact, capable of this car, capable of buying it, owning it, and driving it. That my father could have this car, or would even want it to have it, told me more about him than I had previously known.

I kept the glowing green arm of the dial right on the nose of 25 as we eased down a small side-street.

"Now if you ever get pulled," he said, "you turn the car off, and you get out. You get out and you walk to the cop, and you meet him in the middle, right between your two cars, so you can talk to him like a man, face-to-face." My father looked out the window, rubbing his bottom lip. "None of this standing-over-you, flashlight-in-your-face bullshit," he said. "You let him know that you expect to be treated like a man.

And if he wants to give you a ticket, fine. But you take it from him standing up."

"That doesn't sound right," I said.

My father turned on me, suddenly furious. "That's what my daddy told me, and I *saw* him do it," he said, which seemed to place the theory beyond debate.

I shrugged, and I spun the wheel of the car again. It spun like it wanted to spin, the car carving a simple line in the road, the relationship between my fingers and the tires unobstructed and direct.

This was a Japanese car, back when such a thing had an obscurely exotic feel—a smooth V6, not a piece of shit Ford or backwoods Chevy but the finest machine the Japs had ever put out, although my father had recently dialed back calling them "the Japs" once he'd been accused by a few coworkers of buying a rice-burner.

"He couldn't stand them," my father said. "My daddy just couldn't *stand* the police. And I'll tell you what it was. It was that he knew them," he said, his voice rising. "He'd known them growing up. Knew them and he knew *their* daddies. Had worked with them. Saw them every damned day. And he knew the lot of them were a bunch of no-account hillbilly fools!" By now my father was nearly shouting, jamming his finger in the air to emphasize his point. Then he pulled himself up short. For a few moments the car hummed quietly beneath us, the darkened storefronts outside ticking by one-by-one until, finally, my father pulled his finger into his fist. The anger drained away from his face, and he sat back in the seat.

He was a younger man than I am now, his salt-and-pepper hair combed up high off his forehead, his body squat and strong. The Naval Academy ring he always wore, a tremendous gold piece embedded with a green stone the color of a nighttime jungle, lent a weight to his pronouncements that they otherwise lacked outside the confines of his car. Indeed in everyday life my father was a quiet man. He was deferential and pleasant. It was only inside his vehicle that he found space for a genuine expression of his otherwise closeted self, as though he had beaten a retreat back into privacy from something that had scalded him and driven him away.

"Turns nice, doesn't it," he said.

"It does."

"It's pretty," he said quietly. "It's a pretty car."

"It is."

"Well," he said. "Your mother won't drive it. She thinks the seats are too hard. She told me to take it back."

"Are you going to?"

He frowned, he shrugged, and he flipped the fingers of his hand out straight beside his face in an indication of something that would perhaps be familiar to no one other than myself.

I think the root of the problem lay in the fact that every four years, from about the time he was sixty until the day he died, my mother's father would buy a new Cadillac. My grandfather was a large and rich and rangy man, with a long face and a straw Panama hat that he wore cocked in such a way that made wearing other hats in other ways seem childish and ill-considered. He always bought a black Cadillac, and he always bought it from the Chevrolet dealership outside of town run by a man who had cut my grandfather's grass as a child. When my mother told this story, as she often did, she was at pains to emphasize, with deep solemnity, that her father paid with cash. Her daddy paid for cars in cash. It was the sort of ringing axiom that transcended meaning, insisted upon as it was before I understood how cars were bought at all, and that it might be considered unusual to pay for cars in cash, unusual to do so every four years, and certainly unusual to do so for Cadillacs. But those cars were silky, wide, and low-slung. As a child I'd watch my grandfather ease his long frame behind the steering wheel and drop a little Nat King Cole on the tape deck, a little Ink Spots. He'd ease the thing out into the street like it was a yacht backing out from the slip and then he'd roll down the window and hit the backroads at an even 65 that felt as easy as shit through a goose. That was my mother's father, little like my father's father, and less so still like mine.

So when my parents returned from our own local dealership in moods of poorly concealed rage, I can't say I was surprised. I was huddled over my homework in the kitchen when my mother threw open the door and strode across the room, stack heels ka-thunking on the linoleum, head held high as she slammed the door behind her. It was a look and a walk that she would adopt when in the midst of an important decision, when deeply and fully involved in the task at hand. In later years I would come to align this sort of behavior in others with something like righteous indignation, with fury and a promise of hot revenge, but in my mother and on this day I knew only that she had tagged along with my father to go out to the dealership and pick up the Legend. My mother had insisted on going because she wanted to get out of the house. Because she wanted to see the car for herself. Because she didn't think my father would get a good deal. Because she didn't believe my father would be able to handle himself with the salesmen. Because my father was not her own father.

A few moments later my father pushed open the door, and he stepped into the kitchen. He stood by the refrigerator and slowly unzipped his blue windbreaker over his round belly, and as he did so he shook his head, and he whispered to himself. I stepped past him and looked out into the garage where I saw two cars, the bodies of two cars, the engines still ticking in the half-light of the overhead lamp. It took longer than I thought it would for me to identify them, to recognize them for what they had always been.

"You didn't get the Legend," I said.

"No."

I walked back to the table and sat, and I watched as my father looked around the half-lit room, struggling feebly with the zipper at the bottom of his jacket.

"Your mother," he said. He pulled at the thing. He put his chin to his chest and he pulled again and then pulled the other way and then finally yanked out the zipper with a sound like the tearing of a wet rag, ripping it completely away from the jacket. He threw the jacket off one shoulder, then the other, and then he pulled it around in front of him and grabbed at it with both hands and balled it up to the size of a grapefruit, and he hurled it against the chair. Then he stood there, looking at the thing, daring it to move. The jacket obeyed him for an instant (and then another) before it slowly, almost teasingly unwadded itself, and slumped lifeless to the floor.

My father took a deep breath. Never once looking at me, he put a hand on his knee and he leaned down, picked up the jacket off the ground, and held it out before him. He ran a flat hand down across it, smoothing the material, then he folded it over his arm. Folded it again into thirds. He folded this into a neat rectangle, which he lay with exaggerated purpose over the back of the chair. He placed his two hands on the chair and leaned forward, looked down at his shoes, and pushed out a long breath.

"Your mother," he said, standing back up. "Enjoys that a little too much."

"Enjoys what?"

"Speaking," he said, "with the dealer."

"What happened?"

"She walked out."

"She did."

"She didn't like the numbers we'd settled on. So."

My mother came back into the kitchen on slippered feet, her scarf and earrings gone, her lipstick faded, the blush on her cheeks rubbed out. She was now a good deal less radiant, a little more human, perhaps even fallible, and yet that humanity remained limned by just the faintest line of a white rage that was, even as I watched, fading away like cooling coals. She walked past my father and cleaned the kitchen table, placing papers, mail, various stacks of nonsense on the kneewall.

"They'll call back," she said to the work under her hands.

"Yes ma'am," my father said.

"They'll call back," she said.

They called back.

When my father asked me to come with him to help pick up the car, I knew that the offer implied that my mother would not be joining us and, in which case, I agreed. It was never clear to me how the car was finally bought, how a number was settled upon. I had, and still have, no idea how my parents spoke to one another, an ignorance that has not served me well in later life. These conversations, and everything else pertaining to their relationship, were to me elements of a larger drama of the civilized world with which—given the simmering bitterness it had instilled in my own father—I never desired nor expected to engage.

It was late by the time we got to the dealership. The place sat up on a hill in the middle of an otherwise gray and empty field, the inside of it lit up like a birthday cake. Huge overhead fluorescents shone down on the white-tiled floor, and ten-foot windows hung on three walls like black mirrors looking blindly onto the road below. Every so often someone—staff, dealers, mechanics—would walk quickly through the showroom, sheets of paper in their hands, faces set, like figures passing through a train station in the middle of the night. Doors would open and shut around corners. Steps. Doors. Silence.

While my father met with the salesman (a man,

his age, balding), I found myself down a side hallway studying a small wooden plaque hung with little brass plates. Highest Grossing Salesman, it said. Leesburg Honda. A door clicked shut somewhere behind me. I turned. Nothing.

I turned back to the plaque and leaned in close. Chris Branson, it said. 1980. Chris Branson, 1981, 1982. Kalim Mansour, 1983. Ah. A usurper. A wandering Arab. Wandering in and taking out Branson. Taking out the three-peat champ. Got to wonder about the office politics there. What was it like for Kalim? Out here. In 1983. Michelle Simpson, 1984. Simpson, 1985. Kalim Mansour, '86. Look out Michelle. Here he comes. He's up off the mat. A man like Mansour isn't going to fold. Isn't going to fade. Isn't going to just turn his face to the wall. Not after beating Branson. That prick Branson. Do you have any idea what Mansour's been through? Before he even got out here? This is the end of the line for Kalim Mansour. This is his last stand. Simpson, '87. Damn. Mansour, '88. Simpson, '89. Mansour, '90. Mansour, '91. Cheryl Winston, '92. Cheryl Winston, '93.

I checked back over the list, picturing the salespeople as their names would have them. I imagined them moving back and forth in that empty and well-lit place, stomping around the desks with their smiles and grudges and suits and scarves. I stared at the empty space, not yet filled, for 1994. For '95, '96, '97.

Empty spaces to hold the same acts yet to be registered, acknowledged, and displayed. And those acts would be so registered, and in perpetuity, out into a time that had not yet come and yet was no different from this one. Was its double, or its echo. Out and out, for as long as people wanted cars. Forever.

I turned as a woman passed me in the hall. She was older and well-dressed.

"Excuse me," I said.

The woman stopped and turned and faced me. She was a big woman: big bones, wide shoulders, a head full of frosted hair. I watched her face register something like surprise and then—was it amusement? Curiosity? Something for which I had no word, and in that moment I didn't want to stop and consider it because to do so would've frozen the question in my throat.

"What happened," I turned back to the plaque, "to Kalim Mansour?"

The woman looked to the plaque and then back to me, her face moving from incomprehension to indifference and then back again to that first and curious smirk.

"You really want to know?" she said.

"Sure."

She squinted up her eyes in the darkened hallway and leaned in to look at the plates. "Kalim," she said, mouthing the name slowly. "How many times?"

"Six," I said without looking.

"Six."

She stood back up to her full height and looked down over her shoulder. "Come on," she said. Then she moved past me and opened the office door next to the plaque and walked inside, leaving the door open behind her.

I looked down the darkened hallway, listening hard for anything, for my father or for the salesman my father was with. I looked back into the office. The angle was such that I couldn't see the woman or where she had gone. I looked back at the plaque, a dark and mute square of wood and tin.

"It's a good story," her voice called out.

I walked into the office.

"Do you have a girlfriend?" she asked.

The woman was sitting behind a long, dark desk scattered with papers, contracts, Post-its and carbon sheets, yellow and white and pink. Her red coffee mug sat cold on a corner. Reading glasses lay by an obsidian paperweight. A Diet Coke. The woman was leaning back in her chair, smiling.

"What's wrong?" she said.

I sputtered out a laugh. I adjusted my seat.

"A boy like you I'm sure has a girlfriend," she said. "Even if you don't call it that. They probably don't call it that anymore." She reached for the coffee cup and took a noisy sip. "You probably get lots of attention. Lots of little girls following you around."

"No," I said. "Not really."

"Well," she said. "It's not your looks. So what's the problem?"

"Well."

"C'mon," she said, sitting forward, still smiling. She put down the cup and folded her hands on her desk as though this moment were a scene of negotiation, or contest. "Look," she said. "Maybe I can help. I used to be a girl myself, a long time ago."

"It's nothing," I said.

"Girls can be tough," she said.

"Ha!" I laughed again, and I looked around the office.

She leaned a little further forward and she squinted up her eyes. She was old to me, but younger than my mother. Nothing like her at all. Not a girl, not a mother. Another creature altogether. "Let me tell you a little secret," she said.

"Okay."

"Let me tell you what girls do."

"I thought you were going to tell me about Kalim Mansour."

The woman stopped, and her lips drew back into a smile both wide and false. She grabbed a pen off her desk and sat back and clicked the button repeatedly with her thumb.

"Kalim, Kalim," she said slowly, shaking her head at me as though that name were mine. She looked back at the cup where it sat and then back to me. "You know," she said, "he could've used some of this, too."

"Some of what?"

"I mean, it's all tied up together," she said. She crossed her legs and picked up the cup, took another sip and looked at the ceiling. "Men that are," she sighed, "unsettled."

"Men are unsettled?"

"Most."

"Kalim was unsettled?"

"No question."

"What was it that unsettled him?"

"It's—." The woman stopped, and her face closed up like a fist. Only her eyes moved, and I could tell those eyes were judging not so much me as this moment in which we sat, gauging the seconds of its time as she let them tick off in silence.

Then it was over. "Look," she said, and she leaned over her desk again, bringing us back to that negotiation I couldn't place. "It's simple," she said. "Here's what it is. As plain as I can make it. You get this straight, and they'll be eating out of your hand. This is the secret to the whole thing. It's that a girl," she said, "just wants to be a girl."

"What does a boy want?" I asked.

"What does any boy want?" she responded.

"What did Kalim want?"

"Kalim wanted to sell cars."

"What did you want?"

The woman raised her chin and a different smile passed her face, one that wasn't false but true, and behind it hung another face altogether that I hadn't yet seen, and then all of it was gone. The cup, the sip, the cup returned. When the woman spoke again she did so slowly, as though she were speaking to someone from another country, another world. "A girl," she said, "wants to be a girl, to a boy. You know how to be a boy, don't you?"

"I think so," I said.

"Well," she said, and her chin fell down into a nod, and she continued nodding slowly at me, or rather at us, at what we two were together. And whatever we were was something that stretched beyond where she and I were sitting and into something larger and much more uncertain, something the end of which remained occluded, darkened, impossible to mark. Then she reached down to her glasses, and put them on.

"Hey," my father said from the doorway.

"Hey," I said.

My father stood there, framed by the door and the dark hallway behind him. His hands were in his pockets, his feet set wide beneath him. He flicked his eyes to the woman and then to me. He looked at my hands and my face, as though to check the status of an invisible circle around my chair, testing whether that circle had been breached. By me, or by anyone else. After a few moments he jerked his head out to the hallway.

"We're all set," he said. "Let's go."

As he turned and left the doorway, the woman lowered her head, and her hands moved to the papers in front of her.

"You never told me what happened," I said, standing.

"What?" she said.

"To Kalim Mansour."

She raised her head. No change of expression. As though a stranger had just walked into her office unannounced.

"Get the fuck out of here, kid," she said, and her eyes turned back to her desk.

I clicked the blinker up and took another turn back onto the main drag of the empty town. My father had been quiet for a while, and I looked down at the speedometer, noticing, for the first time, how far over the needle could run.

"Bet it doesn't really go to 160," I said.

My father glanced over. "It might," he said quietly. "There's no place you could test it," he said, pulling on his bottom lip. "And you see, that's the thing. Where in hell are you going to get a chance to run it that fast? You or I? It's for show," he said, his voice rising again. "And they go and they build the car for it. They sell us precisely what we don't need, and they sure as shit charge us for more than we could ever possibly use." Then he looked back out the window. "They're happy to take it," he said after a moment. "We're happy to give it, I guess."

I rubbed my thumb over the stitching on the gearshift, and I looked at the radio dial, at the climate control, at the chain of black and empty warehouses that ran along the road at the edges of the town before it all opened up into fields and forest.

"Your granddaddy's first planes flew just about that fast," he said.

"Did they?"

"They did," my father said, inhaling deeply. "When my dad started flying, it must've been '42? '43? These little BT-9s. Wouldn't go more than 150 tops."

"How fast were the bombers?"

"The ..." His eyes narrowed out the windshield. "You're talking about the Douglases," he said. "They didn't go more than 220, I don't think. And that might sound slow, but those things were built to dive. Climb up into the sun and drop like a hawk." As he continued to speak about his own father, the sound of my father's voice slowly evened out, calming itself into something patient and plain. "The amazing thing," he said, "was how they got those planes to take off from the decks they had on the carriers back then. Eight hundred and twenty feet on the deck of the Yorktown. You're taking a three-ton prop plane carrying a two-ton payload. Plus gasoline. A quarter of the time it wasn't even enough to make it back. More than once he had to ditch it."

"I didn't know that."

"Yessir. Battle of the Philippines. They sent him out to chase the Japanese carriers on retreat, out past his range. On the way home he had to ditch over the water in the middle of the night. Ditch the plane and parachute out and tread water and wait for the York-town to show. Just floating out there with the sharks."

"Did Nana know where he was?" I asked.

My father's face crinkled up at the question. "Well. No," he said. "Well, she knew he was in the Pacific. Pacific theater. But there's no way she could have ..." He gathered himself and tried again. "No one woman knew more than any other," he said, "about where they all were."

The town and its lights had fallen away, and we were out now in the frozen country, nothing but blacktop between us and the next town 15 miles west. I leaned on the gas.

"But I think about that a great deal," my father said. "What that night must've been for him. I think about if the water was cold. I think about if it was choppy. I think that if you're alone in the dark and wet to the bone and no one's out there, you've got to start to think that maybe nobody's coming. That maybe you've been cut loose. Been left behind."

When I saw the red and blue lights reflecting on the fields around us, I at first believed that it was a trick my father had somehow organized, something he had rigged for me as a test or a game. Or perhaps the lights were for someone else—another car pulled up ahead or an emergency in the next town that demanded immediate attention. But after a few moments, it was obvious to both of us that we were the emergency, that we were the ones getting pulled, that the cop coming up fast was out here on the road tonight for us.

I looked down at the speedometer, which, as we'd talked, I'd run up over 85. Then I looked up at the rearview and then over at my father. His eyes were narrow on the road in front of us, his face set in deep concentration.

"All right," he said quietly. He said it as though this moment were both expected and inevitable—had been foreseen and was part of something larger that had now come to pass.

I thought about the car underneath us. I thought

about the V6. I thought that if this thing ran as fast as a plane that it could get us away from a yokel cop. That I could jam the accelerator into the floor, and it would just be me and my father blasting out into the dark. That thought ran down my leg, and it coalesced there like another skin on the sole of my foot where it lay tensed above the gas.

COYOTES

My friend recently came back from a trip to L.A., where he stayed in a house with a deaf and blind dog. They called the dog Roomba because it roamed through the place bumping into things and scarfing up food. It was old but not tired, and had settled into a steady rhythm of life that it seemed it could sustain indefinitely. But my friend wanted to tell me about the dog so he could actually tell me about the coyotes.

The coyotes roamed the edges of the neighborhood at dawn and dusk, big-eared, serene, drawn tight as bow strings. Coyotes love to trick domestic dogs, to play with them and draw them away from their yards and out into the hills where the pack can turn on them, kill them, and eat them. From this time-tested game, Roomba was immune thanks precisely to his handicaps, so at six or so every afternoon, he'd patrol the fenced-in backyard with his nose to the ground, blissfully unaware of the coyotes darting in and out of the brush on the other side. I have to imagine those animals were curious—perhaps even frustrated—that their natural charisma, their superior athleticism and streetsmarts and dark and exotic draw of the wild had absolutely no effect on the snuffling trash compactor who labored diligently just feet away.

I don't know about L.A., but when I lived in San Francisco, I used to run out in the Presidio by the Golden Gate Bridge. It's all pine trees and crumbling cliffs dropping off into the pounding sea, and, as the park is generally empty, the place is a runner's dream. There's wide honey-golden routes that run you past the main attractions, and then narrower paths out to wilder places—to beaches you wouldn't otherwise know existed, to unannounced art installations in the woods, to old bunkers and rusting ballistic missile sites and radar towers surrounded by barbed wire, gray paint peeling in the wind.

I once found myself down one of these side paths that then opened up into another and another, until after a while the track was just about as wide as my own foot and nearly overgrown. The further I ran back into a grove of eucalyptus, the more I wondered if I wasn't on some sort of water runoff or deer path, and soon I found myself in a part of the park I'd never been in before. The dry leaves of the high trees rattled against one another as I came to a clearing—no underbrush, no scrub—and here the trail petered out completely before a circle of what could only be described as beds, as worn indentations in the grass arranged in a rough half-circle before me, each one about three feet long. They looked like little nests, and I wanted to bend down and touch one—just brush it with my fingers. But I knew it was better to keep my feet, better to keep my hands free and my legs beneath me, just in case they should decide—against their nature but still—just in case they should choose to come at me all at once.

Coyotes come across the Golden Gate Bridge at night, lured by the smells of the city, and they're not the only ones; the city's got cameras on the thing, so they can tell. You've got possums and raccoons and skunks and deer and snakes, but it's not at all unusual for mountain lions to pop over at night for a dumpster dive, nap in the park for the daylight hours, then head back over after the sun goes down.

Roomba's limitations saved his life on a regular basis, but the local coyotes weren't so easily dissuaded. They had watched their prey and learned its habits and had taken to killing squirrels and mice and hanging bits of the carcasses on the fence for Roomba to find. The owner had seen the meat himself, pink and bloody and flecked with bits of bone, woven into the black chainlink like a prank.

"God knows how they get that crap into the fence," the guy said, "but once those fuckers set their mind to something, they tend to find a way."

A NON-SMOKING HOUSE

It was dumb luck that I got introduced to Patterson. He was about ten years older, and spent most of his free time at the bar out in Fairfax where my girl worked, a big and hippy button-nosed waitress whose attraction to me was mysterious but not unprecedented. She was also, without question, my type—the type that feeds her Eggo to stray cats and takes the three-legged dog home from the shelter. Some might say I was taking advantage of the girl, but when you're the only white man sitting on the curb outside 7-Eleven in the 15-degree dawn with those fresh-off-the-boat Hondurans waiting for a fat man in an over-sized pickup to offer you a gig ripping out AC ducts or hauling trash, you stop worrying about what's best for everybody else.

I'd spent a fair amount of time in construction, especially the independent contracting that was Patterson's bread and butter. My girl told me Patterson had work, and when I pulled up a barstool next to him, he said that this was so, his eyes on a day-old copy of the *Post* crossword puzzle. I offered up my services as calmly as I could, and I knew that even though the job wasn't enough to set me straight—it wasn't the answer—it would do. I was just about old enough to know that there was no answer. I was 23, and I was dead tired.

It was eight o'clock when Patterson and I had set up at the job site, a big old Victorian not a half mile from the Metro. It was early for us, what with McDonald's for the breakfast muffins and then Home Depot for the nail clips and pry bar on account of Patterson misplacing his own. If you've never had the pleasure, Home Depot first thing in the morning is not a place for the casual shopper—not a place for the guy that's looking for a can of deck stain or a pack of lightbulbs. Home Depot first thing in the morning is a serious place full of serious men, quiet and desperate men trying to get over. Salvadorans, Guatemalans, those hard-as-nails Hondurans, and the occasional grizzled white dude in a stained T-shirt with fear plastered all over his face because he knows the day already balances on the edge of defeat.

I'd been on the job for about three weeks, and Patterson and I were well past the honeymoon phase—that had lasted about 20 minutes. We were now into the part of the relationship where he was trying to get me to quit so he could say I'd been given a fair shot. I could see he hated working with someone else, but I could also see that this Victorian was a two-person job, and he was behind for the month, maybe for the year. For as much as he didn't want to show it, I could see that money-fear stamped across his forehead as clear as a brand.

We found the pry bars and were on the road by seven, which put us almost smack in the middle of rush hour. This wound up Patterson even more, the miles per gallon of his powerstroke diesel dropping like a stone in the bumper-to-bumper traffic. Gas was up to three dollars by this point.

"From Purcellville to your house is twenty minutes," he told me, "and I can't do over sixty with these cops down every access road."

"I know it," I said.

"Every single access road. They're all night catching the working man coming home from the bar and they're all morning catching the working man humping into town."

"I know it."

"From your house to Home Depot is another ten, then out to Arlington is forty-five. At least. You do math, don't you?"

"I do."

"So that's—"

"A lot."

"An hour fifteen," Patterson said, fiddling a cigarette out of the pack jammed down in the cupholder. When Patterson was pissed, he uncorked one of these little diatribes against the local football team, the federal government, particular women, whomever he was sitting next to. And he was pissed more often than he wasn't.

"You mind if I bum one?" I said, watching his thick fingers handle the cigarette. I'd made myself quit based on the cost of the things, but Patterson smoked like a furnace, and his whole vibe had me itchy.

"Buy your own damn cancer," Patterson mumbled as he lit the cig in his cupped hands, his knees pressed up against the wheel. He took a drag and sat back, and the diesel jumped underneath us as he stomped down on the gas. "Hour fifteen out, hour back," Patterson said. "I'd kill a man to save the fifteen every day." He turned to me with the glowing cigarette stuck in the corner of his mouth. "I'd kill him graveyard dead."

I was running the boxcutter down the top of the baseboard molding when Patterson's Nokia started to chirp, echoing around us in the empty room. I tried to ignore it and focus on the job at hand. There's real pleasure in the first steps, in taking a house apart piece-by-piece, especially the sections that lock into place when you first put them down. All you've got to do is lean into those bits just a little, and they pop right out like a rotten tooth. You get the razorblade started with a little wiggle into the caulk, and then there's this suggestive drop as it falls down behind to that space you had to know was there to find. After that you've got a long and slow and even draw all the way down to the corner of the room, just like opening a present.

"Yes," Patterson said into the phone. His voice was soft, like he wasn't sure what was wrong, but he was ready to claim it.

I figured he was speaking to a woman, and one whose opinion he valued.

"And you're right," he said. "No." He put down the nail gun and looked at the floor. "You're taking the dog," he said. He ran his hand up his forehead and pushed back his ball cap. "Where are you? Hello?"

Patterson took the phone away from his face and held it in front of him like he'd never seen it before. He flipped it closed and stood, and he walked to the far wall and reached out and grazed it with his fingers. Then he walked over to the window.

"That bitch," he said quietly, and he turned on his heel and started running across the room, his hand reaching back behind his ear and drawing into a fist.

When Patterson punched the wall it made a sound like a bell wrapped in a mattress. His hand bounced off behind his head, but that hardly slowed him down. The next four punches tore open the drywall like wet paper, the chunks of gypsum collapsing with flat little coughing sounds.

Patterson shook his hand out at his side and stood back to look at what he'd done. "Sonofabitch," he said. He raised his hand in front of his face, grit his teeth, then stretched out his fingers until they shook.

"Shouldna hit the stud," I said.

"Goddamnit," he shouted, holding his hand at his chest and walking in circles around the room.

Patterson shook out his hand again and stuffed it in the pocket of his shorts and pulled out a lighter with the trembling tips of his fingers. He somehow managed to light another cigarette.

"Going to be tough getting in work today with a broke hand," I told him.

He glared at me. Then he dragged out his Nokia again. I could hear it ring. I could hear it go to voice-mail. He flipped it closed and shoved it in his pocket. He pulled on the cigarette until it squeaked in his lips.

My girl's friends at the bar had told me he was divorced. Recently so. They told me he lived alone in a big empty house in the woods on a decent stake of property, just him and an enormous dog. I'd seen the dog from time to time sitting in the back of Patterson's pickup outside that very same bar. A big yellow lab. I've always believed that the dumber the dog, the happier he seems, and Labradors—being the dumbest of all dogs—have discovered the Zen secret to the simple joy of life-as-lived. Patterson's dog looked to be about the dumbest Labrador I had ever seen. One afternoon on my way into the bar, I saw Patterson standing by the bed of his truck, putting his forehead up against that dog's and talking to the thing, rubbing the white fur at the hinge of its jaws. It just stood there, huge and stupid and mute, while Patterson whispered to it, its tongue flapping between them in the air.

"So, she took the dog," I said.

"Fix that wall," Patterson said as he walked over to the window.

I told him to clean up his own mess, and I bent back down to the molding. The best part was the next part, when you had to pull out the nails with the pry bar, just so. I slid the nose of the bar down into the slit I'd made with the boxcutter, careful not to touch the wall behind it and make a mark as indicative of incompetence as any in contracting. The pressure necessary to pop out the seating of the nail was variable but predictable—like finding the friction point in a stick shift—and deeply satisfying. I looked up to see Patterson overtop of me, one hand still holding the other at his chest.

"You do what I say," he told me, his teeth clenched around the cig. There was anger in his face, but it was mixed up with pain. I could tell he was wounded, and probably not a little afraid, so I pulled the pry bar free of the wall and was bringing it up to his face, just to show him, when we heard the downstairs door open.

"Hello?" A woman's voice. "Hello?" A lower octave. Jagged. Older. "Patterson? Patterson, where are you?" I hadn't yet met the owner of the place, but I knew for certain who had just walked in.

Patterson stood up, his eyes wide. He turned to the open doorway behind us, and then he pulled the cigarette from his mouth and handed it to me. "Take it," he whispered.

"And do what?"

"Take it. This is your fuck-up."

I watched him and I didn't take it. He dropped it on the floor between us.

"Patterson? Are you upstairs?"

"Just getting started," he called out. He was pointing at the boxcutter, his eyes round and white. "Cut the wall," he said.

"I'll just come up," she said.

"No, I'll be down."

"I'm already coming," she said, annoyed. Hard-soled shoes started up the stairs.

"Cut the fucking wall," he whispered, pointing at the coffee-cup-sized holes where his fist had been, and then he was walking out of the room, shaking his hand at his side.

I picked up the cig and the boxcutters and opened all the windows and turned on the box fans and threw the cigarette out into the grass.

Over the roar of the fans, I could hear them out in the hallway. Her voice was sharp, persistent. Patterson's voice hummed back at her.

"I just wanted to swing by and see where we were," she said. "I wouldn't have expected you to still be working on the bedrooms."

Hum hum.

"Well you're on my way, so it just makes sense to drop in, doesn't it?"

Hum hum hum.

"I'm sure you're very busy, Patterson. You've got a lot of work here to get through."

I ran over to the busted wall and traced a rough

rectangle around the holes.

"Now, where are you with the upstairs bedroom?" The echo to her voice was gone. They were right around the corner.

"We've just now started," Patterson said.

"Why do you think it's taking so long to finish the bedrooms?"

"I gotta be honest, we're ahead of schedule."

There was a pause. A good five seconds of nothing but the fan blades running through their cycles.

And then this: "Whose schedule?"

"Ma'am?"

"Do you have some other schedule that contradicts the contract?"

"No ma'am."

"Do I need to see your schedule and compare it to the one we both agreed on?"

"No ma'am."

"I have a lot of work, Patterson. A lot of work around town, and I need a competent contractor who can complete it on budget and on time."

"Yes ma'am."

"Don't make me ask you where I could find one."

I popped the thin blade into the wall and bore down with steady pressure, cutting in little stops and starts. Too much force would draw a slice down to my waist before I could rein it back in.

"Why don't we see where you're at?" the woman said.

"Well, there's not much to see."

"Let's just see."

Down. Turn. And back across the other way.

"Oh," she said as she walked into the room. "Oh."

"It's a two-person job, ma'am," Patterson shouted over the fans.

"I'm not paying any more for two people," she shouted back.

"No ma'am."

"Did you say no?"

"No."

"What?"

"I'm— "

The woman shooed Patterson away with the back of her hand. She was somewhere past sixty, and dressed like she was on her way to high tea. I could tell in two seconds that she had the real money, had probably been running this hustle and dealing with pricks like us for decades—and it was also obvious that she enjoyed this, enjoyed her anger and its righteous deployment against the help. She wore sunglasses inside. A scarf on a summer day. As she waved her hand around the room, the silver bangles on her arm slid up and back.

"Has someone been smoking?" she shouted.

"No ma'am."

"I smell smoke. I wouldn't want anyone smoking in here."

"No ma'am."

"This is a non-smoking house."

"Yes ma'am."

"What is he doing?"

"Rotten drywall," I said over my shoulder.

"What did he say?"

Patterson walked over and turned off the fans. It had no effect on the volume of her voice.

"What did you say?" she shouted across the room.

The cut was finished. If you'd had a level and slapped it down all four sides, that bubble would've laid true in the green and stayed so. I clicked shut the boxcutter and slipped it into my pants.

"Rotten drywall," I said, popping the cut-out onto the floor. "Sometimes water can get caught down the backside and swell it up. Got to remediate out a patch, otherwise it can spread."

The woman stared at me, and then she turned to Patterson. "Remediate out," she said.

"It was faint," I added, "but you got to catch it as soon as you can."

The woman didn't move from beside Patterson, who stood looking at me like a man at the bottom of a well. She was waiting for me to say something else, waiting for me to talk too much. I knew what I looked like to her. I just kept standing there with the cut drywall at my feet, looking like that.

"Thank you," she said finally. Then she turned back to Patterson. "I imagine you'll start on the bathroom by this afternoon," she said, and walked out into the hall.

"We've got to frame the closets," he called out after her.

"You haven't framed the closets?"

"We still need the wood."

"I've paid you for that."

"Yes ma'am."

"When I come back tomorrow, I need you started on the bathroom."

Patterson took off his hat and ran his fingers through his hair. "What time do you think that'd be?"

Another pause. By this point I couldn't help but smile.

"Whenever I can find a spare second, Patterson. Will that work for you?"

"Yes ma'am."

"I don't have the time to talk about things I've already paid for. The day is full of enough surprises as is."

To be honest she was lucky to have us. I didn't much care for Patterson as a person but he was a fine carpenter. You've got electricians and painters and plumbers but the best work, the real work, is done by the carpenter. He's the one who puts up the bones of the place. He's the one doing honest labor. If you're the carpenter, you start it all, from scratch. You sit down, and you measure. You cut the pieces like you think they should be cut. You piece together the pieces you've made. You put up a thing that wasn't there before, but once it goes up, if it goes up right, it looks natural, and true. There's the way the measuring tape jerks in your hand when it slaps back into a coil, or the way the pencil vibrates against your fingers when you lay a mark across the grain of the wood. There's the smell of the cut lumber and the jump of the gun when the nail drives in, and at the end of it all, you've done something, and it's in front of you, and if you've taken the time to get it right, you've got no reason at all to be ashamed.

Patterson sat quiet in the truck, his busted hand laying in his lap like a dead bird. I looked out at 66 curving in front of us like a scythe and packed tight with traffic. I thought about the things I could've said to him, but I didn't say them. Because here was a guy I needed. A guy I couldn't leave behind or work around or change or fix.

"She took the dog," I said.

"Fuck off."

I figured I'd try again. "Why'd she take the dog?"

He looked out the window and cleared his throat and started looking for another cigarette. "It ain't her dog to take," he mumbled.

"She's taking it to fuck with you." That seemed right. That was behavior I could understand.

"She's fucked with me enough," he said, lighting up a fresh one.

"Can I ask you a question?"

Patterson laughed. He took the cigarette from his mouth and held it out the window. The traffic had begun to break up. "No."

"I've never been married," I said. "So, I've always wondered about this. I want to know when you know it's done."

Patterson crumpled up his forehead, his eyes out on the road. He pulled on the cigarette and tapped the ash into the cold McDonald's coffee cup in the cup holder. He put the cigarette back in his teeth, and he punched on the radio and turned it up loud. Sports talk. NFL camp. I looked out the window as the arguments blasted through the truck. Who'd shown up in shape. Who'd taken the summer off. All of a sudden, Patterson shouted over the noise.

"I never should've in the first place," he said.

"Never what?"

"And I told her that." He looked over at me for the first time. "That's what's so fucked up about it. I told her."

"So why'd you do it?"

"It's just—." He squinted up his face. "Her sisters got involved. And her mother." He took a long drag. "Everybody starts making their own little plans," he said, wiggling his fingers at the windshield. "Shit just starts happening, and you don't have no control over it."

"So, if you told her, why'd she go through with it?"

He pulled hard again on the cigarette. "She thought—." Then he looked over at me, and a sneer crawled up the side of his face. "Fuck," he said. He flicked off more ash and then pointed his finger at me. "I'll be lucky to break even on this gig with your ass dragging along like dead weight. I'd drop you by the side of the road except I need somebody to carry the goddamned lumber." Patterson sat back in the seat and slammed on the gas. "Christ," he said, throwing the cigarette out the window.

I took that exchange as a victory.

"Ten miles to the store," he said. "Ten miles out and ten miles back."

"This ain't straight." Patterson threw the wood back into the bin. He picked up another 2x4 and laid it against the wrist of his bad hand and sighted down the edge. "This one ain't straight, neither." When you throw lumber like that, it makes a ringing sound you wouldn't expect, like a hard, dull gong. "Ain't straight." Clung. "Ain't straight." Clung.

One of the orange-bibbed employees came around the corner, a thin man in Skechers. "Excuse me, gentlemen," he said to us, as though everything today were going completely according to plan.

"This here ain't nothing but a bunch of bullshit," Patterson explained.

"Yessir," said the man. He looked haggard but calm, like he'd been through a hard stretch and just made it out alive. The big, gray hands at his sides told me he was an ex-contractor, one of those poor suckers who punched a timecard for the steady fifteen bucks an hour, but some of those guys still remembered what the job is, and this guy seemed to know what this right in front of him was. I took a step away from Patterson and back into the crowd that had already formed around us.

"I don't think you can help me, no," Patterson said. "I need about 12 straight 2x4s, and you ain't got a single one in the bin. I doubt you got one in the whole fucking store."

"Sir," the haggard guy said, "I'd be happy to help

you, but I'd ask you to watch your language."

"My language?" Patterson stuffed his bad hand down in his hip pocket like he was delivering some sort of ludicrous opening argument. "Watch my language when you've got some cross-eyed retard back there on quality control sticking his thumb up his butt while this whole place goes to shit?" Clung.

Then Patterson was off down the aisle in his flip-flops, unlit cigarette between his teeth. "Is there anyone here," he was shouting now, down in front of the cash registers, "anyone here who knows how to do his goddamn job?" Two more orange bibs came running around the corner, young fat kids, completely unprepared.

"As much money as I spend in this place," Patterson shouted, right on the verge of a state I hadn't seen a man achieve sober.

"Sir."

"You call me sir one more time and I'll shove my foot up your ass."

The haggard guy was shadowing us down and back, and now he took a step forward and opened those big, gray hands. "Buddy," he said, his voice lower, his knees bent, his attitude completely changed. "You need to take a few deep breaths."

Patterson froze, his eyes wide on the man who now slid one of his Skechers just a few inches forward.

"You're scaring everybody," the man said. He indicated with his chin the crowd gathering behind him. "Look," he said. "You're scaring the women."

Patterson's face scrunched up like tin foil. "Fuck you," he shouted, and he started walking toward the man, who then quickly backed into the crowd, his big hands held high and open, his lined face slack.

By this point the orange bibs had Patterson surrounded. Employees of all ages and ethnicities—a veritable melting pot of forces—had aligned to contain him. The dads with lightbulbs and housewives with garden hoses had indeed all stopped their shopping to watch as everyone started to move in a little closer, but not too close. All I could think of was news footage of a wild animal escaping the zoo.

Patterson was nearing a full panic. He was bending at the waist to scream about lumber, his broken hand shoved deep down in his shorts. Two cigarettes spilled out of his shirt pocket and bounced on the concrete floor.

"None of you motherfuckers has any idea what a pile of shit this place is," Patterson shouted, then he turned at a rep and feinted at him—an older man, short with a white mustache. One of the fat kids tried to grab on to Patterson's back but jumped away at the last second, baring his teeth.

I heard a rep behind me say something about the police.

"This is the last time for me," Patterson said. "This is the last time."

I walked up through the circle and came straight at him. His back was to me but he could hear my boots on the floor and he turned. I made sure my back foot was planted and I got enough of my hip into it, and he's taller so I gauged for it and I caught him right in the chin. His hat and sunglasses went clattering up the aisle.

"Motherfucker," he said, and grabbed me by the shirt.

Patterson leaned back and tried to connect with his good hand but my arm was in the way. I got my shoulder up in time so he only hit my ear, which still stung like a sonofabitch. We had each other's shirts and were circling around like dancing bears. My foot crushed and slipped on a cigarette. I gave him a quick punch to the ribs.

"Motherfucker," he said again, and took out his bad hand and pushed me with both.

The cash register caught the middle of my back, and Patterson let go of me as I fell to the floor. A woman screamed. The circle had moved around us now, with Patterson's back to the bay doors. His eyes were wild with the fight, and I couldn't tell if he got where this was all going.

"C'mon," he shouted, trying to ball both his hands into fists. "C'mon."

I moved in low toward him and grabbed his shirt with my left while his broken right came down on my shoulder again and I came up and got him under the chin. Not too hard but just enough. Patterson leaned forward and held on to me, his face in the crook of my neck, and I felt two quick taps from his open hand on my ribs, the sort of thing you'd see wrestlers pull before throwing one another into the ropes. I swung him toward the doors and he swung along with me, breathing hard into my neck as I pushed him into daylight, holding on to his shirt just to make sure he didn't fall.

By the time we were out of the loading bay's shadow and into the sunlight, Patterson had turned completely and was sprinting to the truck, cackling high and wild as his flip-flops spun out in the air and landed on the asphalt beside me. I heard the voices from the doorway but we were fast, and I just made it into the cab as Patterson cranked the ignition and peeled out of the parking spot, pulled hard around the turn, ran the red light at the bottom of the hill, and pow, we were on the interstate.

Patterson cut loose a scream.

"*Yeah*," he said, long and hard, his face lit up with joy. He dropped his bad hand on my shoulder, the pain for just that moment completely gone. "We got them motherfuckers!" He shoved me against the side of the door so hard I was afraid it was going to pop open. "That's my man," he shouted at me, his face red. He looked over his shoulder and then back to me as the truck tore through the lunchtime traffic. "*You're scaring the women!*" he said. "Fuck that old cocksucker, am I right? What do you say, brother? C'mon man, what do you say?"

I looked at him. At that face of his twisted up into something I was sure I was never going to see. I reached up and grabbed the seatbelt and jammed it home and pulled it hard once—twice—until it caught, and then I turned away from him. Because I knew what I didn't want to say.

I didn't want to say that we still had to get lumber. I didn't want to say that we'd need to work all night, and him with a broke-ass hand, to get the closets done by whenever it was they needed them by. I didn't want to say that we didn't get anybody or anything because there's no use in saying that when you're in as deep as you are and all you can do is put your head down and finish the goddamn job. So I just sat there, feeling my ear swell up and staring at the dash with him looking right at me, waiting for me to say something.

And then I turned back. "You know what we need to do?" I said.

"What's that?"

The glow had just started to fade from Patterson's face, an unlit cigarette tight between his teeth.

I asked him for one. He shook the pack twice and he handed it over, the lighter stuck down in the cellophane. I took the pack out of his hand and looked at the pale little butts where they nestled together. I jogged them around and drew one and fished out the lighter, and when I lit the thing, I saw more than felt the old smoke open and roll like a dark cool campfire all the way down into every forgotten nook and cranny of my chest. Then I sat back, and I rolled down the window.

"What we need to do," I said, blowing out smoke, "is go get that goddamn dog."

ROWDY

"I'll tell you how he did it. I'll tell you how he did it right now."

Reese leaned forward and spread out his arms, batting at everyone's knees where they sat in the deck chairs around him. They all giggled and held their drinks to their chests and pulled up their feet as Reese swatted their bug-bitten shins, slapping off a sandal with his waving hands.

"Give me space," he said. "Give me some space if I'm going to get this right."

"Reese!" Meg said, laughing like she didn't want him to stop.

Dusk had turned into a heavy summer dark, and the four adults were still drinking on Jimmy's back deck. The baby was finally asleep, and Reese's and his wife Meg's girls were chasing one another in the backyard, chirping about the lightning bugs they hadn't yet seen. The kitchen was clean and the plates were away and the adults had opened new bottles, adding the drinks they thought they deserved to the drinks they'd needed to get through the day. Reese stood facing them all in the dark, the light from the neighbor's porch tracing his shoulders in a burning white line.

"Back up off me," Reese said, still waving his arms. "Back up off me now."

"You don't want to play with that old man," shouted Jimmy, frantic but happy that Reese was here, happy that this scene was being played out on his back deck, happy to be the host and the participant or even patron of what was shaping up to be one of Reese's vintage performances.

"You could see it in that old man's eyes," Reese said, and he got down into a crouch reminiscent enough of the object of his satire that the women squealed and Jimmy barked out a laugh of recognition. "That's the first thing," Reese said. "And that bastard's got on—you remember this?—he's got on those crotch-hugger shorts and the polo shirt tucked in nice. *And. Tight!*"

"Yes!" laughed Jimmy.

"And you've just got to stand there while he's cussing a blue streak and he grabs your facemask like a goddamned bullring." Reese reached up and yanked an imaginary kid to his imaginary knees.

"Yep," Jimmy said quietly.

"And he's got you," Reese said, "and he just keeps walking. He's dragging you after him over to that one single spot on the field. Because there is a six-inch by six-inch square down there in the dirt where it all went to shit." Reese stuck his forefinger at the wood planks of the deck. "The veins on the old man's arms are standing a good quarter inch out the skin and that finger says that your impropriety occurred right, fucking, here."

"That's right," Jimmy said—louder now, because he wanted the women to know that he knew it, and he wanted Reese to know that he knew it, and he wanted to remind himself that this was the truth of it. This was how things had been.

"That son of a bitch is screaming in my face," Reese said, "and he's hoarse now, and he's up so close on me that I can see that slug of mint Skoal stuck back down in his lip, and with every word of his I'm getting tobacco juice sprayed all across my cheeks."

Reese jumped back into a crouch and waved his hands in a pantomime of that long-gone coach on that chewed-up field. The women pealed out fresh laughter as Reese swiveled his head like a kabuki actor and stuck his tongue deep into his lip.

"You're getting sucked into the B gap," he shouted, *"and the pulling guard is coming down the line and he sees your fat ass just sitting there and he's thinking nothing but fresh meat!"* Reese smacked his hands together, and the women jumped. *"And you've got your thumb up your ass and your mind in Arkansas and to hell with the hospital, son, you're about to get put in the doggone morgue!"*

Reese paused in the midst of the laughter, still deep in character, and he didn't move a muscle until everyone had quieted once again. His wide bug-eyes passed over all their silhouettes where they sat, cross-legged in their foldout captain's chairs. Then Reese stood all the way up.

When he spoke again, he did so with the old man's voice, but now it was different; it was calm, and intimate. "Listen to me, son," he said. "Right now. Right now is when I need you the most." Reese opened his hands. "Now is when I need your help. Now is when we do this thing together. Now, is when you make me a better coach."

Reese and Meg had stopped off for the night on their way up from Culpeper where they'd been visiting family. Jimmy had seen them planning the trip on Facebook and was anxious to reconnect with Reese. The two men hadn't seen one another in nearly ten years, but fantasy football and Instagram pics and quick texts about baseball teams had helped maintain the illusion of friendship, the impression that the two were intimately involved in each other's lives. Jimmy had been so nervous about Reese and his family showing up that he had gotten drunk before they arrived in fear that they might not. But they did show, and Jimmy didn't burn the burgers and the baby was in a good mood and the wives were getting along and the girls were giggling out below them in the dark. The night on the back deck was hot and thick and cloudless, the dim stars set far back in the sky.

"You can't get away with that shit anymore," said Jimmy. "You can't grab a kid by the facemask."

"They'd throw your ass in prison," said Reese.

"No questions, just straight prison."

After high school the men had attended different colleges, Reese going on to become a financial advisor while Jimmy had taken a job bartending that had lasted until he'd met and married Julie, and just this week he'd signed on as the manager of the Outback over in Herndon. To Jimmy, Reese looked nearly the same— a bigger forehead maybe, a little jowly—but Reese's hair was slick and combed, and his clothes were intentional and worn with an ease that suggested a wealth Jimmy couldn't recognize in the Reese he knew. For these reasons as well as others he couldn't quite place, Jimmy had decided to get Reese as drunk as possible, and to that end he'd brought out the high-test liquor, George T. Stagg, 141 proof, nearly impossible to find. If there was one good thing about working in the restaurant industry, it was the ability to get quality booze, and the Stagg bordered on dangerous—heavy with nougat and rimmed in a tinge of straight moonshine. The women weren't interested, but Reese was on glass number three and, as a result, he had the whole group lit up, the whole night right on the edge of going either way.

Reese's wife Meg turned to Jimmy. "Did you play football too, Jim?"

"Oh, yeah," Jimmy said, taking a sizzling gulp of the whiskey and pushing down the realization that she knew nothing at all about him. "Reese and I played together."

Reese waved his glass at his wife. "Meg's the real athlete," he said. "All-state midfielder in high school.

Started three years in college. D-1."

"No shit," said Jimmy.

"No shit," Meg said. "I loved it until I blew my ACL senior year. But our coaches weren't nearly as colorful as what you guys had."

The monitor glowed into life with the crying of the three-month old, Baby Jeb. Julie cursed and put her wine glass down and stood and walked back into the house. The three remaining sat and tried not to listen on the monitor as Julie entered the baby's room and held and hushed him. Jimmy leaned forward and clicked off the monitor.

"I think it'd be a disappointment," Jimmy said, sitting back, "to have a colorless football coach."

"But don't you think it's an act?" said Meg. "Something they just put on to get the kids riled up?"

"Oh, totally," said Reese.

"Well," Jimmy said. "I don't think all of it was an act."

"You think someone honestly behaves like that all the time?" An edge had crept into Meg's voice.

"No," Jimmy said. "Look—"

"I mean," Meg said, "how much of that sort of rah-rah bullshit do you really need to get motivated to go out and compete? Doesn't it just get in the way of your own preparation? I mean how are you supposed to execute if you're scared to death of getting physically abused by your own coach?"

"I think," Jimmy looked up at the night sky. "Look, I think that kids—boys—of a certain age, really respond to a certain type of personality."

"That sounds pretty fucking regressive, don't you think?"

"Meg," Reese said quietly.

"No," Jimmy said. "Now, I can't speak for girl's soccer—"

"I like the way you say it," Meg said.

"How do I say it?"

"You say it like it's a completely different thing."

"Okay," said Jimmy, feeling the blood rising in his face. "So, okay. In your. In your community, let's say, what was the more popular game?"

"Oh, come on."

"No, no, hear me out. Who had to sit on a, a float in the parades and throw out candy to the kids? Who had their games on local TV? Was there a homecoming soccer game? What I'm saying is, what were the expectations around—"

"Careful, buddy," Reese said. "We're outclassed on this one."

Jimmy looked at Meg where she sat with her legs crossed, the globe of her wineglass held high beside her face, the liquid black in the light of the neighbor's porch. Jimmy laughed.

"What the fuck do I know," he said. He held out his glass in a toast that wasn't returned. "What the fuck do I know about it," he said, taking a drink.

"Honey." Julie was at the sliding door. "He's still up."

"Excuse me," Jimmy said. He put down his glass and stepped inside the house.

It had only been three days since the baby had been sick. Three days since Julie'd come into the living room where Jimmy had been flipping through his phone, looking at news, pictures, nothing.

"He's burning up," she'd said.

"Burning up?"

"Like a furnace."

"Okay." Jimmy had stood and followed his wife back into the darkness of the house and down the hallway, not knowing exactly what a furnace was supposed to feel like. Nor did he recognize the white pocket of fear that had opened in his chest like water boiling in a pot.

When he'd held his son in his hands, it wasn't like he was holding his son but was holding instead a small and child-shaped piece of iron pulled glowing from a forge. The baby was shaking with the effort of its screams and Jimmy was suddenly, senselessly furious at his wife. He looked at the child, at the silhouette of the child in the half-light of the room. His wife stood mutely beside him as though he knew what had to be done, and Jimmy knew that in truth she didn't believe he knew what had to be done, but he also knew that she hoped against all hope that he would know or would pretend to know, and so he pretended to know.

"Let's get him into the bath."

"The bath," she said.

"Run the water cold," Jimmy said.

He had heard of this, or read about it or seen it in a headline from a website for an article he didn't read.

Suddenly he was sitting in the white light of the bathroom, a bathroom with its little plastic toys now worthless and hateful and the limp washrags on the side of the basin and all of it lit up like an operating room, his son screaming and purple in his hands, shaking in the clear cold water like a motor inside of him was knocking against his skin. The pealing screams sliced down into Jimmy's brain, and he held his boy in the white and churning water, cupping his hand in the cold and splashing it on the baby's back while his wife knelt behind him on the bathmat, her back straight and her hands on her thighs as the water roared from the tap until eventually, finally, the child underneath Jimmy's hands began to cool.

Tonight Jeb was just a little fussy—a few wheezes, a little rattle. It was as though the bathtub had never happened, and for the child perhaps it hadn't, but for whatever reason Julie hadn't been able to put the boy down since. She had lost her confidence somewhere, and the odd kick or squeal dispirited her, preventing her from seeing the rituals through. Jimmy took the baby from her, still a little warm but nothing serious, and he sat back in the rocking chair.

Before the baby came, Jimmy thought he was pretty good with song lyrics. He thought he knew entire albums front to back, albums he had listened to for decades. What he discovered when he sat down to sing those songs was that he couldn't remember how any of them began. They all seemed to start in the middle somewhere and peter out after the chorus. Most nights he'd settle on Springsteen's *Tunnel of*

Love, side B, but could recall, at best, half of the melodies, only one of the bridges. He ended up humming the same sixteen bars over and over but, still imagining himself a musical savant, Jimmy jazzed it up a bit. He'd lag behind the beat, he'd add a few notes. If he were feeling particularly confident he would, at times, build a new harmony overtop the first few he'd laid down. Tonight it was all of the above, the Stagg singing in his head until Jimmy convinced himself that he'd chosen the wrong career (such as it was), and was in actuality a natural musician, his gift in total atrophy other than these nighttime performances that were, perhaps, of some real worth. And if that were so, then so was he—that is, a man of worth. A man of value, a man doing good and useful work. After about fifteen minutes, the boy was snoring in his arms, and Jimmy laid him back into the crib.

"How's the little man?" said Reese.

"Back down," Jimmy said, easing into the chair, feeling for his glass underneath him with his hands.

"Is Julie still up?" Meg asked.

"Sure," said Jimmy. Meg shifted her legs and stood and walked into the house.

Jimmy found his glass by the legs of the chair and he lifted it and took a burning gulp and looked out at the night that seemed as though it had pulled even further back into the sky. He tried not to notice that his friend's wife had left as he had entered. He tried not to think that he had been a subject of discussion. He tried not to hate her already.

"I'm sorry if I sounded like an asshole earlier," Jimmy said. "Girl's soccer is no joke. The way they run those girls?" He pushed out a low whistle. "I could never have handled that. No way."

Jimmy let that sit for a few seconds and waited for Reese to say something. To say forget about it, buddy. To say it's nothing between friends. Reese didn't say anything.

"You know what I read the other day?" Jimmy said. "Right up the road here, at Park View. Soccer coach, girl's soccer coach. Sleeping with the players. Or one of them. It didn't say." Jimmy waited for a few seconds. "I mean, it's rape," he said, tipping the now empty glass back for a gulp that wasn't there. "Can you imagine?" Jimmy kept on. "I mean, that's the sort of shit," he burped, "you don't have to worry about with football."

Reese sat forward, the white of the neighbor's porchlight in his hair. He looked at the glass in his hands, and then he said, "You're kidding, right?"

"What?"

Reese turned his glass around in the light. "This stuff is rocket fuel," he whispered. "All right," Reese said. "I told myself I wouldn't do this." He sat back and exhaled loudly and he said, "You remember when you got beat down in the JV shower?"

Jimmy opened his mouth. He looked at Reese, at the black bulk of Reese in the chair, and then Jimmy didn't want to look at him anymore. He turned and looked instead down the long and empty deck. The cooling grill at the end of it. The road beside and the field past it and the treeline somewhere behind that. The squeal of the girls in the yard brought the moment back to him.

"Look," Jimmy said. "I was dumb. It was a dumb prank, and I paid for it. Because look," he said, surprised at the intensity rising in him. "I stole. I stole somebody's wallet. Out of a locker. Marty's wallet out of his locker and I got beat down in the shower for it. Probably just like I should have."

"That's right," said Reese. "And the varsity heard about it, and they came in to help. It must've been twenty guys in that shower."

"I mean," Jimmy laughed. He looked away again, and—"No," he said. "No, now, wait a minute. You don't steal, okay?" He was struggling to control his voice. "You damn sure don't steal from your teammates. Those are your fucking brothers, and there's a trust there. There's a trust that if it's broken—"

"I'm talking about what happened."

"What happened?"

"What happened after, Jim."

"Right." Jimmy put his glass back in his lap. He looked back down the deck. Out at the trees in the yard. The night around him hadn't changed. Nothing had changed. "What did you hear?" Jimmy said.

For a few moments Reese didn't say anything. Then he rubbed his palm quickly across his forehead and said, "I mean, you weren't a buck twenty then. Nobody." Reese dropped his hand to his lap. "Look, what I'm saying is …"

Jimmy stood and he walked into the house. He

opened the fridge and popped two cans out of the plastic (one. two. simple.) and he watched the refrigerator door swing shut. He listened to the icemaker cut on, then off. After a minute he turned and walked back across his kitchen and slid open the door and walked back out onto his deck.

Reese had shifted the chairs. His and Jimmy's now pointed looking out at the long backyard and the black mass of trees at the end of it. Reese sat in one with his leg cocked up against the deck rail and Jimmy sat down beside him as he handed Reese a beer.

"You know who I grew up watching?" Reese said. "As a little kid? Tom Landry. This was way back. Coach of the Cowboys, sure, but I mean he helped conceive the game of football. From the beginning. When you're talking about Landry you're talking about the ... the fountainhead. It all springs from him. And what was he?" He turned to Jimmy. "What was Tom Landry?"

"Landry," said Jimmy, confused and relieved. "Stoic. I think he cut a guy one time for laughing on the sidelines."

"I see those kids playing now," said Reese. "Especially the college kids. Pounding their chests and screaming. Slashing their thumbs across their throats. It upsets people. The schools get fined and the networks cut away from it, but the fact of the matter is they'd cut our nuts off if they really knew what it took to play football," Reese said. "And back there at the beginning of it all, there's Landry. Walking the sidelines with the fedora and the sport jacket. Watching boys go after each other like he's watching waves on a beach."

"I remember Landry," Jimmy said. "I remember Landry and Gibbs and Parcells and Buddy Ryan and the whole thing."

Reese gestured at the trees with his beer can. "They came after. They were the children of the beast. They were human and they prayed, but Landry? Do you think Landry prayed? To whom, exactly, would Landry pray?"

"You've lost me, buddy," Jimmy said. "Lost me completely."

"It's this," Reese said. "It's: *Who would let it happen*? Who would start something like that?" Reese took a gulp of the beer and he said, "I'll tell you—and it makes me nothing but relieved that I've got two girls. What it takes is someone who knows what it is, and then goes ahead and does it anyway. There's something evil at the bottom of all of it, Jimmy. Haven't you ever thought about that?"

Jimmy looked at the trees. He took a drink. "About what," he said.

Reese was silent for a few moments, picking at the tab of his beer can. "Jim," he said. "I know we were never close, you and I. But when I think about what they did to you ..." Reese turned his head to Jimmy. And he kept looking as though he were waiting for some sort of acknowledgment, some nod or cry or something Reese thought he would or should see. After a few moments he sat back. "Have it your way," Reese said.

Jimmy stood again and walked back into the house. Hearing Meg and Julie talking in the den, he stopped in the darkened kitchen and stood and listened, and he was struck not so much by what they were saying but by the quiet way in which they spoke. He imagined that they were talking about normal things, and he imagined that they agreed on those things. Jimmy felt himself hope that the two women could be friends, and that their friendship would hold these two families together as everyone grew older.

He put the beer down on the counter and walked down the hallway to the baby's room. He turned the knob and opened the door.

Julie's rough whisper came down the hall after him. *"If you wake him up so help me——."* Jimmy stepped in and closed the door.

In the dark he saw the green light of the monitor clamped on the edge of the crib. The artificial ocean on the sound machine hissed out and back, and out and back, and underneath it, faint but persistent, Jimmy could hear the breathing of the baby in the crib. One breath, and then another. And each one of those breaths fell and rose into the next, still just a little ragged but strong and natural and self-sustained. Jimmy stood in the darkness of the room, and in those breaths he heard an insistence that stretched into a time that lay on the other side of his own. He put his hand down in the dark and it found the chest of the child where it lay in the crib. Jimmy felt the body rise and fall underneath his palm, rise and fall like a thin machine, and full in each of those risings of a thing he did not in truth sense otherwise.

Meg pulled her leg up under herself in the captain's chair, the stem of her wineglass caught up in her fingers. "I mean," she said, "I dated football players."

"Damn straight, you did!" shouted Reese, too loudly.

"I dated football players and lacrosse guys and whatever."

"Not me," Julie said. "I liked the artists. The painted fingernails and the absinthe."

"Well I mean, I was a jock and so were they and whatever," Meg said. "And they were rough guys."

"Really?" Julie laughed. "Oh, you like the rough ones."

"Rowdy," Meg corrected herself with a smile in her voice as the three young girls walked up from the backyard. The girls were all tall and bony, their limp straw-blond hair nearly glowing in the dark. "The guys were rowdy," Meg said, putting her arm around the one that came nearest. "And they were fun and whatever, but what I always saw was this. What I always saw was that the meaner the coach, the worse the team. If the coach was calm and focused and, just a fucking *adult*. You know what I'm saying? If the coach was an adult, the teams always seemed to win. If the coach was an overgrown child, well …"

"We had great teams," Jimmy said evenly.

"Why do you think that was?" Meg said.

"We had the talent," said Jimmy, batting at Reese's leg. "Am I right?"

"Okay," Meg said.

"But look," Jimmy said. "That old man was a motivator. He understood how we worked."

"See, that's what I don't get." Meg sat back. "Who's *we*?"

Jimmy stood up, could feel himself standing before he realized he was doing so. He stood and he waved his hand out at Reese. "You remember his great advice? You remember his words of wisdom? How to be a better man?"

"Get meaner!" Reese shouted.

"Right."

"Get tougher!"

And now Jimmy himself was down in the crouch, his tongue stuck deep in his lip. The two little girls squealed as he shuffled around the porch until he was standing in front of Reese's chair.

"You want to get your dick knocked in the dirt in front of all those hot little pieces of tail up in the stands?" Jimmy said.

"No, sir!" shouted Reese.

"You think you can play for this team with your ass full of candy and your head full of buttermilk?"

"No, sir!"

"What?" Meg laughed.

"I'll tell you right now what the problem is," Jimmy went on hoarsely. "The problem is that everybody's gone soft! Everybody's crying over spilt milk! It's getting so we're all just willing to sit here and take it. Just take it like we've got a big, red, bullseye on our chests." Jimmy stuck his finger into Reese's chest. "Do you have a bullseye on your chest?"

"No, sir!"

He pointed at one of the girls. "Do you?"

"No, sir!" she called out.

Jimmy stood up. "And now," he said. "Now is when the old man changes it up. Now's when he gets personal. Now's when he homes in." Jimmy walked back around to Meg where she sat. He leaned down in front of her to look at her in the dark. "What he does is he finds your eyes," Jimmy said. "And he's looking deep down, searching for a key down there that he can turn. You know what I'm talking about?"

"Okay, Jim," Julie said.

"That key that'll get you to get it. And he gets in close. Close enough for you to smell him." Jimmy began to thump his finger lightly on Meg's knee. "He's got his eyes locked up with yours and he says—and he says it quiet—he says *Son*, he says, *You. Are not. The target*. He says *Son. You, are the bullet*."

Jimmy stood back up. He opened his arms.

"What was that?" Meg said.

"That was it," said Jimmy.

"What was it?"

"That was it for me."

"But you know how stupid that sounds," she said. The girls started to giggle and shuffle their bare feet on the deck. "You know, right?"

Jimmy dropped his arms. Everything was up in his ears. The people and the night and his own fucking booze. "Yeah," he said. Jimmy took another step back. He tried to hold her eyes where he imagined them to be. "I guess," he said.

The monitor clicked back on, the baby's cries raw and fierce and scratchy in the dark.

"Honey," Julie said.

"I guess it was stupid," Jimmy said.

"Honey, I'm sorry, but could you?"

"I guess I was stupid but—"

"But what," Meg said. Her head hadn't moved, nor had her wineglass or the hand that held it. On the blue screen beside her the baby kicked out his white legs once and hard and held them there, suspended in the air, his eyes open and black to the otherwise dark of the room.

SWISS SEAT

The zipline was new, or at least we'd never noticed it
before. It ran through the forest as tight as a wire, tied
way up in a huge oak about thirty yards from the
creek bank. Gallagher saw it first, and indicated its
presence with a stunned gurgling sound in the back
of his throat, coupled with some agitated gesturing at
the branches above. Justin and I stopped, our eyes following the arc of Gallagher's insistent arm, and the
three of us stood dumbstruck in the middle of the forest, our heads craning way back to take the whole
thing in. The line was alien, unplaceable, and in some
way titillatingly rude, stretching out like black mathe-
matics against the chaos of the trees.

"Fuckin-A," Justin whispered, and I nodded my
head in assent.

"Out*standing*," shouted Gallagher, having finally
regained the power of speech. He looked from Justin
to myself with something like ecstasy on his

pockmarked face, then he raised his chin back up to the rope above us. "Out-fucking-standing, indeed."

If the forest had a name, we didn't know it. It started behind the house of a kid Gallagher assured us was a prick (football player—Justin had keyed his car) and went back along an overgrown dirt road for about half a mile. After that we'd drop our bikes and jump over the creek and then take a left up the hill and into the trees that stretched on for as far as we knew. Back then it probably ran all the way out to the mountain. That's cut down now, but this was before it was cut down, before the toll road and the open-air shopping mall and the artificial ponds stocked with fish.

We had all come from somewhere else, and we understood ourselves to be the sole proprietors of the newly dug subdivision that every week seemed to push further back into the woods. We reacted with fury and disgust to every new cul-de-sac we stumbled upon, silent and empty and rung with fresh houses that looked just like our own, houses that were thrown up by workmen in a week, the driveways laid, the straw scattered across dry manure and grass seed. The four-lane boulevard that had originally come to a hard stop at the entrance to our court began to inexorably continue out into what had been those unnamed fields and forest, winding along a route that seemed as predestined as it did obscene—and we three were the only ones who gave a shit. We broke the windows in the empty houses. We threw glass bottles in the freshly laid basements. We walked through the cement before it dried. We pulled up the sapling trees in the yards and chopped the flowers they'd planted in the median. Cops were looking to catch us in the act and we knew it and we were proud.

We determined the zipline was about 60 yards total and secured with a series of knots that impressed even Gallagher once he'd *ascended* (not climbed) the big oak to assess the situation. After ticking off the names of the knots employed in the binding and anchoring of the line, Gallagher told us what we had suspected from the ground: that there was a good-sized platform in the crotch of the tree; that the rope ran down at about a twenty-degree angle to another big trunk on the other side of the creek; that it was tied there with a series of knots that, from where Gallagher stood, looked to have been executed with a degree of professionalism at least equal to what he saw before him.

"Whoever did this," Gallagher said, "is ex-Army. No Marines take the time to rig up something like this. Those dumbasses would just wade into the creek and waterlog their boots and next thing you know is trenchfoot, but who gives a shit anyway cause it's all *next-man-up* for those fucking gung-ho morons. What you need," Gallagher said, calming himself by running his hand over the knotted ropes, "is some forethought. What you need ... is some goddamn planning."

"Fucking Marines," Justin said, sighing as he pulled his dad's Ka-Bar knife out of the holster on his belt.

Marines were no good. It was agreed upon that the Rangers were the ideal outfit. Gallagher could deliver lectures on the topic ad nauseam, and Justin gave it a shot every once in a while, but Justin was just as likely to lapse into the exploits of the Tennessee Irregulars during the War of Northern Aggression. No state had seen more violence during that hateful incursion, you see, than the Volunteer State, and so no population was more familiar, per capita, with the guerrilla tactics necessary to expel invaders. Justin would ramble on while sharpening that Ka-Bar on creek stones, and then Gallagher would chime in with the advantages of the impressive ROTC program at the University of Tennessee, emphasizing how it was essential for every civilian to engage in military service in order to appreciate the sacrifices necessary to live in freedom.

"Israel does it," Gallagher said. "Everybody goes into the army whether you want to or not. That puts some real skin in the game. Makes for a whole nation of trained-up badasses."

"Fucking-A," said Justin. "Mossad."

"What's Mossad?" I asked.

"You don't ..." Justin stared at me. "You don't know Mossad."

"Fuck Mossad," Gallagher said. He was back down at the base of the tree dragging out one of the coils of rope he always carried in his backpack. "It's about Shayetet 13."

"Shayetet 13?" Justin's hands fell in his lap.

"Shayetet 13," Gallagher said. "Better than the

Seals. The Seals, first off, are Navy, so they're queers. Second off, Seals have sold out now, anyway. Bunch of *New York Times* Bestseller List bullshit. But Shayetet 13. Now that's who you bring against the Supreme Leader. That's who's killing the Iranian nuclear scientists. No Title 18 for those salty fuckers."

"Title what?" I asked.

"Christ," mumbled Justin.

"Last week," said Gallagher, "last week this Iranian scientist gets shot walking out of his house. Briefcase in hand. Dead on the front lawn with his coffee cup laying beside him in the grass. Gunman on a motorbike. Black hood. Nobody saw nothing."

"Good for the Shayet 13," Justin said, his eyes back down on his knife blade. "Clean out these fucking ragheads." He struck the knife against the stone a few more times and then looked up and said, "Did you know they marry their sisters?"

"No," I said, shaking my head. "They don't."

"They do," Justin said. "They're allowed to. It's in the Qur'an. They're allowed to marry as many women as they want. Just keep them like cattle, all robed up. It's sick. A whole race of misogynists."

"Not true," said Gallagher, winding the rope around his elbow and thumb, spinning it into a large and growing oval. "Muslims love their women."

"How about Prisha?" I asked.

"Prisha?" Gallagher didn't know her.

"Arga—something."

"Got her in Bio," Justin said. "Second period."

"Hot, right?"

"Too dark. Little tits. But yeah."

"Sounds Indian," said Gallagher.

"What's the difference?"

"She's hot, right?"

"No tits, not interested," Gallagher said.

"She has tits," I said.

"Does she wear robes?" Gallagher asked.

"I don't think she's Muslim."

"No robes, not Muslim," Justin declared.

"Truth," said Gallagher. He tied off the coil and dropped it on the ground and put his hands on his hips. "Muslim chicks need robes because their tits are so big."

"Bullshit," Justin said, but you could tell he was considering it.

"For real," Gallagher said. "Huge. Muslim girls have tits so big that you can't leave them alone on the street. Can't let them go to the store. Can't let them drive a car," Gallagher said. "Tits so big you can't let them open a bank account. Can't even let them buy a house."

Gallagher was smiling at me as he spoke, and I started to sputter.

"Okay, okay, so if you think that," Justin said, waving his knife at us. "No, listen. If you think that, then you've got to admit that the ragheads don't deserve their women. Because I call a race of people that run down their women a bunch of misogynists."

"You heard that word in Civics last week," I said.

"Home Ec," said Justin. "So you know dick."

I looked over at Justin in his Army surplus T-shirt

and his camo pants, the canteen on his hip filled with water for two hours of screwing around in the woods. He shucked the knife down the rock in his palm, tearing up what had to be a sixty-dollar blade. I looked back to Gallagher, who immediately puckered his lips in a silent imitation of Justin's pout. Justin jerked his head up and looked at us both.

"But you'd still fuck Prisha," I said.

Justin bent back down to the knife and stone. "I might be racist," he said. "But I ain't crazy."

I needed some outside confirmation on Prisha, as my feelings for her had recently escalated beyond my control. She sat behind me in Geometry, and she was a little prim, so you had to want to see it, but if you tried—and you didn't have to try very hard but if you tried—you'd catch the subtle way she'd snake her back around when she sat down, or you'd see how her hair would drop straight as a curtain when she'd cock her head to work on a math problem. Or if you just sat back and watched her as she walked up to the front of the class in her plain, simple, everyday pants —wasn't trying to look slutty, wasn't trying to put on a show, wasn't even trying to get noticed, but if you had an eye, a discerning eye I'm talking about, for something the idiots wouldn't notice ...

The fact that she wasn't white already scared off three quarters of my competition, but a few knuckle-heads had started to send her ridiculous notes, which she'd shown me. The occasional imbecile shouted at her in the hallway. As pathetic as they were, I still felt like I had to act fast, but gently. A not-quite-accidental touch, a quick conversation at her locker. Help her with her books. People had sensed way back in the reptile tail of their brains that Prisha was beautiful, but they hadn't quite fully processed it yet, and I wasn't about to help anybody along. Except, I just had.

Gallagher sent Justin back out to his house to get the carabiners and the harness from under the deck, and we watched Justin turn and run back through the woods, crashing through the underbrush with his flat feet and his pumping elbows. "Dumbass," Gallagher whispered. "You know he says his dad was a Ranger? Such bullshit." Then he turned to me, his face suddenly bright. "Hey," he said. "We don't need the harness."

"Why not?"

"I got an idea."

"Should I go get him?"

"Fuck him."

Gallagher took off his pack and rooted around for a second, then dropped to a knee and grabbed the coil of rope at his feet and slung it over his shoulder. He stood and walked toward the tree and moved up the trunk without breaking stride, simple and easy like climbing a ladder. When he got to the top, Gallagher opened his pack and pulled out two more coils and laid them on the platform, then unspooled the rope from his shoulder and knotted it on a branch and spun the other end down to me. By the time I got to the top, Gallagher was doubling up one of the other ropes in his hands.

"It's called a Swiss Seat," he said. "Called that because of the mountaineers." He kept his eyes on his hands as they found the two ends of the rope and then milked them back to the doubled-over center. "It ain't all cuckoos and chocolate out there, my friend," he said. "The Swiss only seem friendly. A foreigner takes one step out of line, and the whole country goes on lockdown. I'm serious. Every road and bridge is rigged to blow at all times. The Swiss are trained with firearms from the time they can walk. Expert skiers," he said. "Climbers. Mountain people for ten thousand years." He held the bit at my hip and doubled it around my belly. "You do not fuck with the Swiss," he said. "You give them your money, and you shut the fuck up."

Gallagher tied an overhand knot at my belly button. "How's that?" he said.

"Fine," I said, faking it.

"I mean is it laying on your fat or your bone? You get it on your bone, it'll snap your pelvis if you fall."

"Fat," I said, still faking it.

Gallagher dropped two ends of the rope to the platform and then spun me around. "This is the tricky part," he said to my back, picking up the ends and running them through my legs. "Get this part wrong, and you'll lose a nut. No Prisha, no nothing." He pulled the rope tight up through my groin and tied the ends to where it ran across the small of my back, then back down through, and he turned me again. "Bisect the back pockets," he said, "of your saggy-ass jeans. You get in boot camp, they won't let you sag your pants. You know that, don't you?" He pulled the ends to my left hip and tied a square knot, fed it through to the right, and tied an overhand. He put his hands on my shoulders and pushed me away to arm's length and admired his work.

The rope ran around my waist, through my legs and back, tracing and retracing a black outline of my pelvis over and through the meat on either side of the bone, an exoskeleton of black nylon looped and fed.

"Swiss as fuck," Gallagher said.

Justin called up from below. He had the carabiners but couldn't find the harness.

"Don't need it," Gallagher shouted back. "Toss up the carabiners."

"He's going first?" Justin called back.

"He's all wrapped in. Toss up the carabiners and quit whining."

"This is bullshit!" Justin shouted. "I got the stuff. I'm going first."

Gallagher leaned over and untied the rope from the tree branch. It dropped with a hiss, thudding into the leaves by Justin's feet. Justin walked away, cursing under his breath.

Gallagher called after him. "We need the carabiners, dipshit."

And then Justin was back. He was looking up at the two of us, and now he was smiling.

"Hey, buddy," he said to me. "Trade places with me, and I'll tell you something."

"Tell me what?"

"About your girl."

"Who's that?"

"Dude. Prisha."

I stared down at the benign and freckled face. I asked myself if I could trust anything he said.

"I've heard some stuff. Your girl ain't what you think."

"You don't know shit," I said, but I'd said it too quickly. The color was already rising in my face. Justin held up his open hands, and he slowly started backing away.

"All right," he called out. "But don't say I didn't warn you." I could only let him go about four steps before I called him back.

"You sure you want to hear it?" Justin said. I was out of the rope harness and Gallagher had started to feed it around Justin's waist while I had stepped back into the corner of the platform to lean up against the tree trunk.

"I'm sure," I said.

"You're not going to like it."

"Tell me."

"This is from Darnell," Justin said, "so, consider the source."

Gallagher laughed.

"Okay," I nodded, but the cold burn had already started in my gut. I knew Darnell. The stories about him weren't stories you wanted to be in.

"So, Darnell says he and Edwin took Prisha into the boys' showers after soccer practice." Justin's back was to me now as Gallagher fed the ropes through the belt at his waist, then down across the back pockets. Justin peeked at me over his shoulder. "Darnell says he didn't even have to tell her what to do. Says she got down on her knees in the shower. She undid their belts. She unzipped their flies. Darnell says that Prisha sucked off the both of them."

"Nope," I said. "No way."

"Had Edwin in her hand and Darnell in her mouth. Just went back and forth between the two of them. Like a pro."

"It's bullshit."

"I'm just telling you what he said."

"First off," I said, anxious to make an argument, "she doesn't even play soccer. There's no reason for her to be there." But she ran track. Four hundred meters. Always wore blue leggings. "Second off," I said, "she would never get with Darnell."

Justin smiled. "Because Darnell's black?"

"No," I said. "I didn't say that."

Gallagher looked up. "Correct me if I'm wrong, but Prisha ain't white."

"Well, she's not black," I said, my voice rising in a way I hadn't expected.

"Why don't you ask Darnell what she is?" Gallagher said.

"Nope," I said, shaking my head. "She's not like that," I said, because she wasn't. But Darnell did, in fact, yell at her in the halls. Just her name. Loud and teasing and sing-songy like he knew something. Then Prisha rolls her eyes, and smiles, and turns into her locker. She puts her hair behind her ear. And there I am standing there beside her, holding her Geometry book.

"All girls are like that," Gallagher said. "They just pretend they're not."

Justin giggled as he watched Gallagher knot a long rope to the harness. "Hey," he said. "What's that about?"

"Okay. This," Gallagher said, holding up the loose end of rope, "is the brakeline. You look down there," he said, pointing out to the far tree at the end of the zipline. "You hit that thing at top speed, and you're going to be in trouble. I can lean into this for the last five meters and slow you down."

Justin had stopped listening. His eyes were back on me. "C'mon," Justin said with a smile. "Maybe it's all bullshit. What are the chances a couple of black dudes would go for a Muslim girl, anyway?"

"Black dudes can be Muslim, too," Gallagher reminded him.

"She's not Muslim," I said quietly.

"I'm telling you," Gallagher said, "it's those hot raghead chicks."

"She's not a raghead."

"Shit, man," Justin said to me. "Don't blame yourself. It ain't even about you." He looked down the length of the line to the other side of the creek. "Black dudes will go for anything."

I stood there and watched him watch the line as it ran down through the leaves. Justin became very quiet as he looked across the creek, and when he spoke again, his voice was lower, heavy, as though it were bubbling up from a deep and quiet part of his mind. "Could you imagine a whole pack of them running loose in some Muslim country?" he said. "They'd have to lock them all up. Bury them under the jail."

"Why do you think the Saudis have such a stick up their ass about their women in the first place?" Gallagher said lightly as he clipped the carabiners onto the Swiss seat. "Think about how close they are to Africa. I'm just saying."

Justin's back was to me where I stood leaning up against the tree, and my eyes drifted down to the tie Gallagher had made for the brakeline. It was just a simple overhand, which I thought was strange for such an important knot. And it looked a little loose. A little sloppy. Then Justin was pushing his butt up against me, getting ready for a running jump.

Gallagher shuffled down to the far end, his hand on the line. As he turned back to us, his face was stern, and he shouted in the seesawing cadence he'd probably heard drill instructors use in movies.

"Outboard personnel, stand up!"

"Fuck yeah," said Justin, and he started to bounce on his toes.

"Hooooooook up!"

Justin clipped the carabiners on his belt to the line.

"Check static line!" Gallagher shook the line in his hand. "Check equipment!"

Justin was close up on me, and I could smell the

dried sweat on the back of his neck. The loose brakeline knot pushed dumbly against the back of my hand.

"Stand in the door!" Gallagher's shouting face was red as a grape, ready to pop, and I didn't so much see as feel my hand do it—that is, push, just so slightly, the bottom tail of the brakeline through its own loosening eye. Not enough to pop it out, but almost. Somewhere in the middle. Somewhere between. It felt like a tiny little loofa in my fingers, like a little blind thing at the bottom of the sea.

"*Go,*" Gallagher said.

Justin screamed out a senseless curse, and he ran off into space.

For an instant, there was a lag. And in that instant I had the distinct feeling that we'd made a mistake. That we shouldn't have been there, or, it wasn't for us. The creek and the trees and the line that ran through it. Gallagher and I stood on the platform and watched as Justin whizzed down and away, shrinking by degrees as he moved through the trellised branches, his ragged scream receding and echoing out into the forest. The line yawed under his weight, the carabiner humming away like a little tin motor.

"Where's the rope?" Gallagher whispered. He bent down and wrapped the brakeline around his fist. "Got to do it slow," he said, and he began to lean, and lean, and lean, and there was no sound to it, nothing dramatic, only a little jump as the back knot on Justin's harness gave way. And then the long and slow and even arc of the brakeline rope as it rose in the air behind Justin in a perfect and senseless crescent.

"Shit," Gallagher said.

It didn't even slow Justin down. We could hear the tension in the line that ran by our heads as he went screaming over the water, screaming toward the far tree, and the screaming didn't stop until he hit the bottom knot hard enough to pitch his legs out and above him, slamming the back of his head into the ground with an impact that sounded like a baseball bat hitting a side of beef. It looked like something that would've happened to a doll.

"Shit," Gallagher said again, and he started to climb back down the tree.

The ground had a dank and black and fertile smell. There was the wind, and a cardinal—sweet sweet sweet sweet—and then every once in a while a crow from far off, somewhere across the creek. I thought about the dead birds I had seen, birds flattened on the side of the road, the dry carcasses burnt up by the sun. I wondered if all birds died by misadventure, the victims of cars and cats and other larger birds. If any just died of old age. If one minute they're chirping in the tree, and the next minute their heart pulls up short and here they come, falling down through the leaves, stiff legs pointing at the sky like tiny little sticks. The cardinal again. The wind in the trees, and then that stopped, too.

"What you hear," Gallagher said quietly, "is that you never leave a man behind. But that's a bunch of B.S. Guys get left all the time. It's not in the Constitution. It's an idea and that's it. It's something people say." He was rubbing his hand in circles on Justin's back where he lay facedown between us. Justin hadn't made a sound or moved since he'd hit the ground, and we hadn't tried to move him. He was breathing, but that was about it. "Grab that canteen," Gallagher said.

I plucked it off Justin's belt and opened it and handed it over. Gallagher leaned down and waved it under Justin's nose where lay in the leaves.

"Justin," he said to him. "Water. You want some water?" Gallagher took a mouthful and handed the canteen back to me, and as he did so, Justin's body began to shake, to tremor as though in the midst of a seizure, the hands and feet rattling in the leaves around us. We both sat still and watched it until it was done.

"It's better than nothing," I said.

"I think if we both just sit here," Gallagher said, but he didn't finish.

Blue jay now. Fierce little things. *Scree scree scree*, like a little baby hawk. It was back further in the woods, settling in for the night.

Gallagher looked up at the line where it ran over our heads. "I just don't," he said. "The knots were good knots."

"Okay," I said. "Listen to this."

"Stop it," Gallagher said.

"No, listen. When he gets up, he's going to be super groggy. We can take turns carrying him back to the bikes, and I can ride home with him."

"Stop."

"I don't even have to bring you into it if you don't want. He won't remember, and we'll never tell him, okay? We'll promise now. We'll never, ever tell him."

As I was talking, Gallagher started to scratch at his scalp, slowly at first and then with increasing intensity, faster and faster with his eyes squeezed shut like he was enduring what his own hands were doing and then he stopped. He opened his eyes and he looked at me.

"Turn him over," he said.

"Why?"

"We're going to unwind this thing," Gallagher said, spinning his finger above his head. "This whole fucking thing."

In just a few seconds, we had Justin on his back, his legs in the air like a baby on a changing table, looping the rope up and around and through. We worked quickly, pulling the harness back out from the waist and then under and back through again. Justin's breathing had begun to clot and gulp, his tongue flapping against the back of his throat.

"We've got to get him onto his chest," I said, but Gallagher dropped the legs and grabbed the knife off of Justin's belt and ran over to the tree. I turned to see him sawing at the zipline that he held steady in his fist.

"What are you doing?" I said.

The rope popped overhead with a dull twang—sucked away from us where we stood, coiling back out across the blackening water. By the time I got up beside him, Gallagher was already working on the masses of rope around the trunk.

"Hey," I said to him. "Listen," but Gallagher kept sawing. I looked out at the forest and then I looked back. "She's Indian," I said.

"Shut up."

I cleared my throat. I looked at Gallagher's shoulders and at the field behind him and then I said, "This one is on me."

Gallagher stopped. He lowered the knife, and he turned. And then he looked at me, and he said my name. And when he said it, he said it with patience and with disgust, like he was talking to someone who had no business being out so late and so far away from home.

Behind us, Justin's body shook again. Gallagher held my eyes for a few moments, and then he turned back to the tree.

When I wasn't watching it happen, the seizures didn't sound like much. It sounded like the wind, or an animal rooting around for food. And there was a part of me, a sick and guilty part of me, that wanted it to sound like footsteps. But it didn't really sound like that at all. It was too faint, too random, and it didn't really stop like footsteps would—it kept going long after whoever was coming would've arrived, would've put their hand on your shoulder and turned you around. And then it stopped.

SIT A HORSE

For reasons that passed all understanding, D.C. 101 was still playing the Chili Peppers in 2006. I had grown up on that station and its loose macho vibe, but once I moved into the city itself, I thought I had no more use for adolescent angst. And then you drive fifteen miles west, and it's like time stopped fifteen years ago. It's still like that.

As I sat behind the wheel of a rental car heading back into Nova, I found myself both fascinated and appalled by Anthony Kiedis, by the gall of that goddamned radio station, by my decision to come out to Virginia at all. I spun down the dial and static warp and half songs shuddered until Terry Gross' smooth contralto filled up the cabin.

"There you are, Terry." I drummed my fingers on the wheel. "There's my girl."

I had gotten caught in traffic coming out of D.C., and I was late getting to Broadlands for dinner with

Simone and Charlie. The AC in the car did nothing to cut the heat from the sun that poured through the windshield and pooled right in my lap, and the bottle of Santa Margherita beside me was already sparkling with condensation.

Simone loved that wine, and I'd bought it to make her happy, because when Charlie and I were together she wasn't happy, but that hadn't always been the case. At one point she and I and Charlie had cut a swath through the city while we were all in grad school, but then Simone had gotten pregnant and Charlie had proposed, and they both dropped out and moved back to Charlie's family's place in Virginia. I felt both betrayal and admiration for them in equal measure, which was to me, at the time, proof of their unimpeachable importance in my life.

I eased the blue and numb and senseless car into a strip mall off of 28, and I shifted into park and looked over at the tinted doors of an Irish pub as I took the baggie of cocaine out of my coin pocket. As I peeled it open, Terry Gross told us, told me, that she was pained by recent events in a distant country, and hoped for a clear and quick resolution to the issues at hand.

"Terry, Terry," I said, looking down at the caked white powder. "What is it you want from us? What is it you'd have us do?"

After Simone had taken Charlie away, or vice versa, I had decided to clean up. No more cocaine was the first thing. Then whiskey, then wine, then everything. I heard that Charlie did the same, out of, I would wager, simple competition, but to be honest I was a little relieved. He'd sold out, after all. Got himself a wife and family and whatever their attendant responsibilities must've been, and the Charlie I knew could be a little excessive—could be, at times, a danger to himself and others, as though he wanted to swim out into the deep water just so he could turn around and watch what he'd done. But god, it could be electric.

I hadn't seen them in almost a year, and in that time I had touched nothing stronger than coffee, but hearing Simone's voice on the phone, low and simmering and reminiscent of nothing so much as a disappointed mother, put me right back on a stool in an afternoon bar in Georgetown after the Redskins had lost again and half the place were my mortal enemies and Charlie was the brother I had never had and the best friend I could never hold onto and I pitied and feared the woman who would keep us all alive. That's all to say that on my way out of town, I found myself driving past the old hookup's townhouse right before the bridge. For old time's sake. For a bit of granddad's medicine.

"Granddad's medicine," I said. My palate was thickening with anticipation, and I loved the way the words felt on the backs of my teeth. I wanted to say it in front of someone, but I knew I didn't want to go into the bar. The inside of a place like that was still stuck way back up in the olfactory. Wet carpet. A Chili Peppers jukebox. What had it been, eight months? Eight months was not a thing. Only I would recognize it as such. And who could, in truth, say what I recognized, and what I didn't?

It's a truism that the first few rails never really feel like anything. That same old memory of snorting pills in someone else's parents' bathroom: chalk and dust. For a split second, I found it impossible to swallow.

Gross laughed, full-bodied, sincere.

"Well, Terry," I said, sitting up, "I gotta be honest. When Granddad quit smoking, he just put it down one day. That's what Mom always said. Just put it down in the ashtray and didn't pick it up again." I cleared my throat and wiped my nose and looked around the empty lot. "But that was a different time," I said. "Those folks were stronger than we are now."

Simone was back in the kitchen boiling pasta. As I walked in, she didn't so much as look up, so I set the wet wine bottle on the countertop and took a seat at the kitchen table while Simone stirred with her face down over the pot.

"I brought your favorite," I said.

Simone glanced over her shoulder at the bottle where it sat gleaming in the sunlight. "Not tonight," she said.

I rubbed my palms on my pants and looked around the kitchen. It was pale and clean and roughly the size of my apartment. "Where's Charlie?"

"He's in the study," Simone said to the pot.

"You have a study?"

Simone put the spoon down on the stove and

wiped her hands on her ridiculous apron. Peaches and apples. And she hadn't washed her hair. Everybody gets older, and then here she is. A few times when Charlie had passed out early, Simone and I had tried to have a moment, maybe even two, but we'd always ended up just holding one another, like we shared something difficult that still didn't bridge the gap. And now here she stood in her big kitchen with her runner's body and looking at me like she already knew everything.

But I could tell she was tired. She was raw and red and papered over and right on the edge of something, like she was glowing with a fever that could kill her.

"What do you think Charlie's doing in the study?"

"He's reading," Simone said. She turned back to the pot.

"How long has he been in there?"

"I don't know. Awhile."

I blinked at her, and I waited for her to tell me what she wanted me to already know.

"He's drinking," Simone said.

I slipped my finger back down into my coin pocket. "Okay."

"The girls come back tomorrow," Simone said to the pot. "They're coming back from my parents, and I don't want them to see this."

"Maybe they should know about it," I said.

"Maybe they should—." Simone looked up at me. "They're three, Gabe. Christ." She turned back to the pot. "I want us to talk to him," she said.

I ran my hand through my hair and looked around

the kitchen. Big copper pots hung behind Simone like bells in a monastery. Where did they get the money? Where did they get anything?

"You're clean for how long now?" she asked.

I looked at her. At her scrubbed and lined and age-less face and I kept on looking until I realized I was taking too long. "It's nothing," I said.

"It's not nothing," she said. "It's not nothing at all."

I could feel the smile happening, and I let it happen. "About eight months," I said. "Give or take."

Simone put her hand on the counter and leaned her weight on it. Her face was turned up at me now, trying to smile back. "He didn't think he could do it," Simone said. "He didn't think he could do it until he saw you do it."

"It's one day at a time."

"Do you want anything? I can get you some water."

I rocked forward on the chair. "Whiskey," I said.

Everything fell out of her face at once. "Jesus, Gabe." It was just the look I had been waiting for.

"It's a joke," I said, and I stood up and slid my finger into my pocket again to touch the baggie and then I rubbed my palms together. "So, let's get after it," I said. "Where's this study?"

We both looked up at the sound of feet stomping around on the floor above. A door slammed and Si-mone jumped and then cursed, furious at her own reaction. The feet got louder and louder until they came rolling down the stairs, and suddenly Charlie was standing huge and sweating and smiling in the kitchen. His Hawaiian shirt was open to the waist, his big hands flexing at his sides. His face looked like he'd been chopping wood.

"Perfect," Charlie said. He grabbed the bottle of wine.

I stood up to shake his hand, and Charlie pulled me close and squeezed my ribs until I could barely breathe. Then he turned and dropped a hand on Simone's shoulder.

"Honey, what was it you needed at the butcher?"

Simone didn't say anything.

"Ground pork, right?"

"Yes."

"Ground pork." Charlie turned to me. He leaned in and squinted up one eye. "Aren't you a fucking mess," he said. "I'm driving." Charlie walked past me and pushed open the screen door and walked out onto the deck. By the time I caught up to him, he was already behind the wheel of his minivan.

"So," Charlie said. "How's your love life?"

"Like you give a shit." I fumbled for the seatbelt as Charlie cruised through a stop sign, the wine bottle locked tight between his thighs.

"What is it this month," Charlie said. "A big blonde? All hips and hair? Something you can really dig into?"

"This feels like a setup," I said.

"You know which one I liked?" Charlie was twisting the screw of a wine key down into the cork. Of course he kept a wine key in the car. Or his pocket. It didn't matter. Squeak, squeak, squeak. "You know which girl was my favorite?"

"Melissa," I said.

"Little firecracker."

"Melissa had a ton of problems, Charlie."

"Of course she did!" Charlie shouted. He ran his hand across his mouth. "And *your* problem," he said, "was that you couldn't appreciate it. You were no help to her at all."

The day was high and blue, and the two-lane road wound out from the subdivision and down toward a creek lost in trees. Charlie put the bottle to his lips and pulled on it like water as we drove across a stone bridge and back up into oak-lined streets, Charlie pushing the minivan hard into curves, the tires squealing absurdly beneath us. I gripped the handle over the door.

"You're drinking again," I said.

Charlie glanced over to me. "Don't make me empty your pockets," he said. "I'll grab you by your ankles and shake you senseless. And don't try to change the topic. This is about your failure, not mine."

"What is?"

"We're here."

Charlie lurched to a stop in the parking lot of a low brick building. I sat stone still and watched as Charlie jumped out of the seat and hustled down the sidewalk. Once he had gone inside, I dug with my finger and fished out the baggie and furiously looked around the car for a place to hide it.

I clicked open the glovebox and tossed the baggie inside, where it landed with a whisper on top of a 9mm pistol. I narrowed my eyes and peered back in. The gun was so dark as to be invisible. It was like a gun-shaped void, a chunk of antimatter lying on top of a Geico insurance card.

I reached back inside and plucked out the coke, then closed the glovebox. I sat back in the seat and felt my chest rise and fall and rise again as I looked out the passenger window. The day was cracking open just like it used to, flattening out and sliding like panes of glass. Of course it was worth it.

Charlie jerked the door open, throwing a packet wrapped in butcher's paper on my lap.

"We've done our duty," he said, cranking the car. "We deserve satisfaction."

"I'm not going to a bar," I said. "I won't do it."

Charlie sat back in the driver's seat as the minivan rumbled, and he looked at me. "Got anything you want to tell me?" he said.

"Like what?"

"Like anything you want to share?" He watched me as I sat there and tried not to grind my teeth. "That's right," he finally said. "You never share anything."

Then he pulled the bottle from inside the door and took a drink and set it into the plastic cup holder between us. The minivan clunked into reverse, and Charlie spun back out onto the road.

The first few rails had, without question, begun to rise up. Nothing malevolent, but things had ground down into a new kind of focus as the minivan continued to swing and push. The empty child seats rattled in the back seat as the trees shuddered past us in the sunlight.

"You remember the camping trip with Melissa?" Charlie said.

"Are we back on her?"

"I told you not to change the topic. The camping trip."

"You mean the one with the rain."

"The fucking hurricane is what I'm talking about! All night, right? All fucking night. And your girl ate way too much of the acid and ran around from tent to tent talking about Jesus. You remember?"

"I do."

"He's not there to save us," Charlie said in a high and mimicking voice. *"He's just there to let us know that we can be saved."* He rubbed his hand on his chin. The road swung to the left and the minivan swung along with it.

I felt remarkably light. Translucent. Only the seatbelt across my hips held me down. I suddenly remembered what it was that I was supposed to be doing. "So what started it this time?" I asked.

"Here's something people forget about camping in the rain," Charlie said. "You've got to set up your tent fly tight, I'm talking guitar-string tight, otherwise the water's going to pool on the roof of the thing and start dripping down on you while you're sleeping. Condensation, is what I'm saying. Drip drop. Drip drop."

"Is everything all right with Simone?"

"And the other thing is the groundsheet. You've got to roll the edges of the groundsheet up underneath the tent itself. If you don't do that, the rain's going to collect on the edges and it'll all slide up underneath. You don't roll up that ground cover you'll wake up in a soaking fucking mess."

We drove past the bar I had passed on the way in, so I reached down and punched on the radio. It was already tuned to NPR, and *Marketplace* was on.

"Fucking Kai Ryssdal," Charlie said.

I turned to look at him. Really look at him now as he drove. He had less hair than I remembered. Heavier. Red-faced. A full beard in the summertime. Like a bear hunched over the wheel of a car.

"I mean, come on," Charlie said. "He's lying to us. That slick-haired son of a bitch gets on the radio and he lies to us. Every goddamn day."

It was meatballs and spaghetti, the dining room table set for three. Simone had a big basket of garlic bread and a salad with fresh cucumbers and Jersey tomatoes that she'd grown in the backyard. They smelled like tomatoes and tasted like tomatoes, and while I cut them on the kitchen counter, Charlie kept drinking and talking.

"Rothko used to say that if you didn't break down crying in front of one of his paintings that you just didn't get what was going on. Here's a guy who preached socialism and painted pictures you can't understand without a PhD. Something you probably didn't know: He read the book of Job. Incessantly. His wife left him at 65. He killed himself at 66. I mean, who waits until they're 66?"

"How old are you?" I asked.

Charlie took a gulp of the whiskey and water he held in his hand. "Hey, honey," he said. "We've got a comedian. Gabe thinks he's Jackie Gleason. Do you think Gabe is as funny as Jackie Gleason?" He took another gulp. "I don't think Gabe is as funny as Jackie Gleason."

"Pasta's ready," said Simone.

I went into the bathroom and locked the door. I took out the baggie and tapped out a good long rail on the sink with my face so close to the porcelain that I had to hold my breath. The first few lines were a hello how's it been. A welcome back. But this one. Boom. It opened up some things. Like it's the first line. The first line was nothing. The first line was the empty line. The line that inaugurates the idea of the line. The line that will contain all other lines. So the second is the first. The third the second. And we move forward into an idea that has always been waiting. This one was good. Cold. Frost that's dense like sand.

I helped Simone set the dining room table and lay out the food. I put the bowl of meatballs on the table-top, and Simone picked it back up to put an oven mitt underneath it, and I fell deeply in love with her for three unbearable seconds before it melted away.

I took the seat across from her, and I got ready. Not the first time she and I had confronted Charlie.

Not by a long shot. Or rather not the first time I had been present for a confrontation. Not the first time my presence and its accompanying silence worked like some sort of verification between them both. But they would hold together. Because they always had. I was for them a witness. I hadn't yet learned what they were for me.

I rocked my butt against the wood of the chair. I put my hands flat in front of me, one on either side of the plate. I breathed slowly and listened to that breathing and I rolled my neck around on my shoulders. Simone looked down at her empty plate. Out the window. At her fingers.

When Charlie came in, he had the pistol in one hand and a bottle of Old Granddad in the other. He pulled his chair out with two fingers and set the bottle beside his plate and the pistol beside that. All the lights got lost down there in the gun, sucked in and held there by its shape. Simone picked up the bowl of pasta. She served herself and passed the bowl to me.

"You afraid of bank robbers, Charlie?" I said. "Comanches?"

Charlie gulped his whiskey. "Gleason's funnier," he said.

"What's wrong, honey," Simone said quietly, spooning the meatballs onto her plate.

"I'm in a lot of pain," Charlie said.

"What exactly is causing all this pain?" I asked. Jesus Christ. I could taste tears running down the back of my throat.

"It's whatever," Charlie said. He spun the top off the whiskey bottle and refilled his glass. "You don't have a family, Gabe. I can't talk to you."

"I have a family, Charlie." said Simone. "You want to tell me about all your pain?"

"You can't see it," Charlie said. He took the pasta bowl and teased the long noodles onto his plate. "You never have."

"I see a drunk." Simone's voice was pleasant and even. "Right here in front of me."

Charlie turned to me and whispered loudly, "My wife thinks I need help."

"I'm here to help," I said. The dining room had begun to break up around us all like an eggshell, and Charlie's big red face hung right in the middle of it.

"I'm talking about somebody good," Charlie said. "Like Tony Robbins good. A big chin. Serious."

"Have you thought about going to church?"

Charlie leaned forward. He searched out my eyes and found them. "Judge not, young man," he said. "I've brought a gun to dinner. What's the matter with you?"

"What you need," said Simone, "is some self-respect."

Charlie sat back and smiled. "Yes," he said. "Here we go."

"You need to start acting like a man for your family and your wife."

"Honey, please," Charlie said. "We're Democrats."

"I need to know how this started," I said. "If I'm

going to do anything at all, I need to know how this started."

"Charlie got laid off last week," said Simone, her eyes on her husband. "Now he wants to put on a show."

"What was the job?" I asked.

Charlie spoke through a mouthful of food. "To be completely honest, it's the girls. Isn't that right, baby? We've talked about this. It's the girls."

Simone moved her hands to her lap. "Don't blame them for this," she said. "You don't get to blame them."

"You don't have kids, Gabe, so let me explain. When you have kids, a little part of you—no, that's not right—a big part of you, dies."

"That can't be right," I said. I had begun to sweat. I could feel it up in my scalp.

"No, it's worse," said Charlie. "What happens is that you vanish overnight. You wake up, and you're somebody completely unfamiliar. But here's the catch."

"You're a piece of shit, Charlie," whispered Simone.

"That person that you don't know? It's who you've always been. And man, that's the real kick in the pants." Charlie put down his fork. "You see, I'm almost at the point where I can't pretend anymore. A part of me died when they showed up, and I'm not sure if it was a good part or a bad part, and they're three years old and they're fucking beautiful. Okay, now this is where she cries. Don't cry, honey. Don't cry, baby, please. Listen, our kids are beautiful. They're so beautiful I want to set the house on fire. Nothing I've ever done is worth ten seconds of them." Charlie took another drink and then picked up the pistol. "These kids look at me," he said.

"Your kids love you," I said. The air of the room was burning my eyeballs.

"Now, right there," Charlie wagged the gun at me. "That's the problem."

"Charlie, if that's loaded," said Simone.

"They do love me," said Charlie. "And they've got no idea what a piece of shit I am."

"You're not a piece of shit," I said. It was true. My teeth vibrated with the truth of it.

"Present company would disagree," Charlie said, and he put the nozzle of the gun to the side of his head.

Simone caught her scream in her hand.

"Charlie, it's the girls that are the proof," I said. "They make you good. You're good because you want to be good for them."

"That's," Charlie started to laugh. "That's some real Tony Robbins shit there, buddy. You're not Gleason, you're Oprah. I've got Oprah over for dinner." Charlie had started to cry. "I could use," he said, "I could use a new car."

His chin was quivering underneath his mouth, his enormous arm still holding the nozzle of the pistol that was so dark I couldn't see it to his temple. It was like the pantomime of a suicide. Not even a play but a rehearsal, the props locked away or not even bought. Simone's hands held on to her chair, her arms locked straight, her back rigid, ready for blastoff.

"I see someone who wants to get better," I said. "You can get better if that's what you really want," I said. "Anyone can."

Charlie was now fighting for and losing control of his mouth. His lips blubbered, wet and loose, and his breathing became ragged. He leaned forward, as though he had something to show me.

A sharp crack came from upstairs. Charlie turned and looked up, and we all three sat in silence for a few moments, our plates steaming on the table. Then the crack came again.

Charlie sat back up and held the pistol at arm's length and popped out the magazine, pulled back the slide and racked it out of the frame. He put all the pieces on top of his napkin, and he put his hands on his thighs. He took a deep breath, and then the crack came again.

"You'd better go," said Simone.

Charlie stood up and drained his glass. "Gabe," he said, "put together a plate for me. Mom's hungry." Charlie walked over to the stairs. He stopped there at the bottom for a few moments, looking at his sandals, then he started up.

This was the day the sun wouldn't die. The sky kept moving to catch it and the trees shook inside of it throwing shadows on the bathroom wall like a procession, like a cavalry, like kids throwing rocks at jackbooted soldiers. Good God.

The room rose up or the darkness drained away, and after a few moments I could see my face in the bathroom mirror, my nose pushing out dimes of fog on the glass. I glanced down and brushed off a few white grains from the edge of the sink. This was a new bathroom. The upstairs bathroom. It was gorgeous. It was clean, long and blue, gleaming with chrome that hummed over white beadboard and the plate of pasta sat cooling on the top of the toilet seat, the meatballs cut into quarters. Voices bubbled on the other side of the locked door. The pasta had been chopped up into bits, as though for a child. A mother cutting pasta for a child in a restaurant. His fat face orange with sauce, his fingers clotted with sauce.

The bathroom door shook with the force of a fist.

"Gabe," Charlie shouted. "Where's the fucking food!"

I followed Charlie down the hallway, the plate of pasta held out in front of me like a sacred offering. As we both walked into the yellow room at the end of the long hall, I could see flowers standing in a vase on the TV stand. In the far corner, a lace comforter lay over the single bed. In the middle of the room sat an old woman, reading a book.

"Hey, Mom," Charlie said. He stood just inside the door and crossed his arms.

"Hey." The woman glanced up for a moment, then looked back down to the book in her lap. She wore a pink button-down with a heavy blue blanket over her legs. A small AC unit roared from the far window. The temperature in the room had to be in the 60s. I crept in and sat in a highbacked chair in the corner.

"Need anything?" said Charlie. He looked at the books that lay in a disordered pile on the floor.

"I don't know what time you people eat," she said.

"This is Gabe," said Charlie. "He's here to help me."

The woman took off her glasses with annoyance, and she blinked at the two of us. "Who are you?" she said.

"I'm Gabe," I said, raising the plate of pasta.

The woman's eyes fixed on me, and she lowered her chin. "How are you feeling today, Gabe?" she said.

"Good. I feel good."

"And you're here to help," she said, nodding.

"Everybody needs help," I said.

The woman leaned over her book and put her elbows on her knees. She gestured at Charlie with her glasses in her fingers. "Don't concern yourself too much with that one," she said. "He's past help."

"I don't believe that," I said.

"He's like his father," the woman said, sitting back. "And his father was like him, too. And probably just like Willie and Bucky." Her eyes were locked on to me now, desperate to make me understand. "It's a poison that gets passed down," she said.

"How does it get passed down?" I whispered.

The woman put her glasses back on. She looked out the west window where the sun winked in and out of the leaves, then she turned back to her book. The AC wound on and on in the otherwise silence.

"Mom," said Charlie. "You just said that I was poison. What did you mean?"

"Jesus," the woman said to the book. "Why say a sick thing like that?" She shifted her legs and the big blanket fell off to the side, revealing a pale stretch of her thigh. Then she looked up. "Did she make the pasta again?" the woman asked.

"You mean Simone?" Charlie said.

"You know who I mean."

"She did."

"I don't want it."

"It's what we're all eating."

"She can't do the sauce right."

"Mom, it's your recipe."

"And she doesn't get it right." She looked over to me and said simply, "She doesn't get it right."

"I thought it was great," I said.

"You don't know shit," the woman said. She looked up to Charlie. "Your father wouldn't've eaten it."

"You remember how Dad was," Charlie said.

The scowl of the woman's face melted into indecision and then slowly reformed itself into a smile. She closed her book and turned back to me and said, "I remember the day we married. That hideous little church. Do you know what your father said to me?"

"Who said what to who?" I asked.

"Your father!" the woman shouted. She shifted the blanket back across her legs.

"What did he say?" said Charlie.

"He said he was always afraid his son was a queer."

I bit my lip not to laugh. There was no reaction from the other two. I knew suddenly that I needed more coke. I set the plate of pasta on the floor and picked up the picture frame on the end table and stuck my finger back into my pocket but the baggie wasn't there. In the picture frame an old man held a fish by the mouth. He had enormous sunglasses on his face.

"So, he wasn't worried anymore?" I asked.

"About what?" the woman said.

"Was he a queer?"

The woman leaned toward me, her eyes suddenly fierce. "That man could sit a horse," she said. "Do you know what I mean?" Then she smiled. "I mean, he could sit a horse."

"Was he poison, too?" asked Charlie.

She closed her eyes and shook her head quickly, as if to clear it. The blanket fell back off her hip. "It's this goddamned heat," she said. "It comes off the river all summer long, and we just don't get a break." The woman opened her eyes again, and she focused on her son standing in front of her. "Hey," she said. "What's with that face?" she said. "C'mere."

And as she said it, she tilted her head down and dipped her shoulder. She looked up at Charlie and blinked her eyes with the wide and even smile of false teeth and I stared at her thin white shank as it lay mottled on the chair beneath her.

"Mom," said Charlie, "it's time for us to go."

The woman rolled her eyes. "Be that way," she said, pulling the blanket back. "Just tell Charlie to come by when you see him. He never comes in anymore." Then she gave us a wink. "Charlie hates his mother," she said, opening up her book. "Which is just as well."

"Why is it just as well?" I said, standing.

She peeked back up over the rim of her glasses. "Thank you for bringing the food, son," she said, "but we have all the help we need." As I stood in the doorway, I watched her eyes lose their focus once more and wander to the window. Her hand touched the side of her hair. Then she turned back.

I woke on the couch in the living room. The back of my head felt like it had been hit by a baseball bat, and I sat up to see the two twin girls standing in front of me, side by side. One—was it Riley? The one blond and the other brunet. Riley and Zoe. Their chins sat on their chests. Their eyes were wide, their mouths like little bows. Chubby cheeks.

"Why aren't you in the tent?" Riley asked.

I touched my forehead with my fingers. "What?"

"Daddy put up a tent," said Zoe. "You should've slept in it."

"You should've slept in the tent," said Riley.

I stood and walked past the twins and into the kitchen where Simone was frying eggs.

"Good morning, Gabriel," she said. Outside a thunderstorm was coming down in sheets. It could've been any time at all.

"Where's Charlie?"

"Where do you think he is," she said in a completely different voice.

I looked out the kitchen window to see Charlie out there in the threshing rain, jamming a long tent pole through plastic sheeting. He would push it through a few inches and then it would get caught, the connection would break, and he'd have to pull it out and start all over. The rain whipped down on him in the yard, the limbs of the oak trees swaying in the wind.

"It wasn't loaded." Simone looked up as she pushed the eggs around the pan. "It never is," she said.

After a while Riley came into the kitchen. She asked Simone to read her a book, and Simone told her to go back into the living room. Riley was the loud one. The one that always wanted your attention. The other one, Zoe, she was quiet. She would walk up to you and grab your hand and not say a word. Zoe was the one you could trust.

"Gabriel," Riley said, "would you read us *Fox in Socks*?"

I looked back out at the man in the rain. I started to laugh. I tried to swallow it, but I couldn't.

"Are you okay?" Riley said.

"Your daddy," I said. I tried to finish, but Simone slammed the pan down hard on the stovetop.

Riley didn't even turn her head. "You have to read it as fast as you can," she said.

THE FIRE

I could smell it before anything else, my mother says. I woke you both up from your naps. I didn't know what it was, but I knew it wasn't right.

My mother still likes to talk about the fire. She asks me if I remember how the neighbor pulled my sister up off the grass as she was crawling toward it. How she couldn't decide whether to turn the garden hose on the flames or on the roof and settled for the roof. How they figured out later that some damn fool had dumped ashes from a grill into the middle of the field behind the house well what the hell did they think was going to happen if you dump a fire on top of dry grass, my mother says, as though she's never asked me the question or it has never been asked before by anyone and she is still, some thirty years later, waiting anxiously for a response.

I do remember it. I remember everyone's voices dialed up to an unfamiliar pitch. I remember the flames reaching higher than our home and the black smoke reaching higher still like waves in an ocean that kept rising and not quite cresting. I remember the back of a neighborhood boy as he swatted a rug at embers that had floated down into the yard.

And I remember sitting on the couch afterward—I have no idea how they finally put the fire out—as my parents walked through the house with the elderly neighbors.

Tell me if you smell anything, my mother said to the old man, Hunter.

Woman, Hunter said, my sniffer's long-since broke.

Everyone laughed at that, and then laughed again, and then they couldn't seem to stop, the sound building until it was pealing out in great, hysteric jags. I dug my fingernails into the couch as the adults convulsed in front of me, hands on one another's shoulders, faces red and torqued as they held one another up and barked into their fists and staggered past me and on into the kitchen. And then everything went quiet. I took a breath in the silence, and inched forward on my butt until I could just see my mother through the doorway, smoothing her dress with slaps of her palms, and wiping the water away from her eyes.

RIVER WEATHER

The first time Cynthia didn't come home, Terry sat out front all night, looking down into the forest. He started with a six-pack of Miller and then moved to the vodka and then, even though he said it was against his better judgment, he took out the whiskey. And he went on to say that he always knew that it was going to come to this, that he'd known it from the start. I asked him what he meant, and Terry pulled on the whiskey bottle that he held in his fingers by the neck like a beer and he said that every woman settles for the man she chooses to marry. He said that the tears of the wedding day are in all truth tears of doubt. Terry said that each woman consoles herself with the notion that she can, somehow, in the final act, bring her man around. That night, he ended up sleeping in the lawn chair.

At that time I was sleeping on the couch. When not actively drinking with Terry, I would help out on his contracting gigs. "Apprentice carpenter," was the appropriate title—not that anyone other than me gave a shit. And yet it was a job I was proud to have, because even though I'd grown up in the house of an engineer, I had learned nothing about even the most minor of home repairs. To watch my father turn a five-minute job concerning the screen door into an afternoon-long aria of fury and disgust had warned me off all manual labor, which, given the company I increasingly kept after dropping out of college, had begun to make me something of a pariah. I knew nothing about my fifteen-year-old Honda except how to fill it with gas. I knew so little about driving a nail that I didn't know you had to know how to drive it straight. Terry taught me how to drive it straight, meaning he berated me until I figured it out. And he taught me how to hang a door, how to seat a toilet, how to install a window and a showerhead, and how to countersink a hole to make the screw sit flush so the painters wouldn't cuss you after you got done.

And when we got done, usually around three or four in the afternoon, we'd head out to the Black Dog or down to the Lightfoot Grille and get a reuben and enough beers in us to start to call people and tell them we were going to have a thing out at the house on the hill. This was back when everyone knew where the house was, but that house is gone now, as well as the hill it sat on.

It was Cynthia who had found it abandoned down a dirt road in West Virginia—a beautiful two-story wood-beam with a creek-stone fireplace. And it was Cynthia who'd paid the movers to break it down onto flatbeds and reassemble it on the land outside of Round Hill that she'd bought with the money she'd made in real estate. She and Terry would, after the requisite three-to-four cocktails, regale me with all sorts of stories about the place, such as that it had served as a hideout for Mosby's Rangers at the end of the war, that those long-ago guerrillas had stashed payrolls from Union trains behind the walls, that one fine day the ghosts would return for their reward! That kind of crap.

But it wasn't long after the two of them moved in that Cynthia started to change her mind. The wind in the trees sounded wrong at night. The west-facing kitchen was bitterly cold. After sunset you could stand at the picture window in the living room and look out across the fields and not see a single porch light. If someone was coming up the driveway after dark, you could sit out front and track their head-lights for a solid mile as they drove up through the trees, which was where Terry and I both stationed ourselves with enough alcohol to float a pirate ship that night Cynthia never made it home.

It was right about this time that a man from Qatar bought the forest. That's what I've since been told, down at the Lightfoot Grille and out at the Black Dog. He was a unique addition to the regular, mildly xeno-phobic crowd that frequented these establishments, and as such was all the more suspicious and alluring. There was, for instance, no solid agreement on how to pronounce the man's country of origin. Ka-TAR, some said. You could also say Kwa-TAR. Some went so far as to call it Kya-TAR. What does jibe with my own experience was that the man in question was remarkably tall. Very thin. The sort of delicate bone structure that leads one to just-so-slightly stoop, regardless of ceiling height, as though out of an unconscious solicitude long ago imprinted on the muscle memory. It was also said that he had long, hazy fingernails. A head full of beautiful black hair. *Luxurious* was a word that was used.

What was also agreed upon was that this man had come out to western Loudoun and, inside of a single month, just thrown down an absolute fortune on real estate. Anyone past Leesburg who had anything worth selling seemed to have a deal going with the Qatari. In fact it seemed as though he had put a price on nearly every piece of land north of Route 7, halfway to Winchester. The extent of his holdings stretched nearly to the river, as though he were one of the long-vanished gentleman-planters of old. There was, at the time, very little out that way. Fallow fields, long stands of old trees. Dirt roads. A few houses. Terry's place.

Jorge was making a fuss before Terry even made it off the porch.

"You afraid to play a real game, big man?" Jorge shouted. "You afraid to get beat down at your own house in front of all your white friends?" Jorge stood at the edge of the driveway and pulled out a wad of limp bills and held it over his head.

Heads turned from all over Terry's backyard. Forkfuls of barbecue froze in the air and beer cans were set to the side as Terry kicked open the screen door of the side porch with a gin and tonic in hand. He looked like a ballplayer gone to seed, which he was: thick shoulders with a beer gut and a crumpled Budweiser baseball cap over his sunburnt face.

"I'll take my rich friends over your mongrel ass any day, Pablo," Terry said.

"It's Jorge, motherfucker."

"Not out here it ain't," Terry said, and walked gingerly down the wood steps, his cocktail held out to the side for balance. "It's my rules out here, son," Terry shouted in order to remind everyone whose house it was and who was allowed to raise his voice. "And if you play it straight, you're gonna lose all that cash you got by cheating natural Americans out of an honest day's work."

The mothers had led the children to another part of the yard, and the men laughed into the backs of their hands while Terry walked past Jorge without even looking at him, fiddling a Newport out of his shirt pocket.

"The aborigines," Terry mumbled, "are starting to get uppity." He bent down and picked the horseshoes out of the grass, then he called for Mo.

"Hey, Mo!" he said. "We got a live one here."

Mo was over at the grill testing the pork butt. I liked Mo. He was big, a head taller than anyone else, and his arms were as thick as thighs and covered with ink. His square beltbuckle spelled out FUCK.

When Terry called for him, Mo didn't turn. He just leaned forward and gently shut the top of the grill. Then he reached back with his thick fingers, untied his apron, folded it into an even square, and laid it on top of the cooler. He took off his stiff black ball cap and dug in his pocket for his roll of cash, peeled a twenty off the top, dropped it in, and tossed the hat to me. While Mo began to swing his arms and puff like a furnace, I passed the cap around to the fifteen or so men who had gathered up around the horseshoe pit. The bills just poured in for Terry and Mo.

Jorge had brought a lean dude with him. There is no other word for this man other than *dude*—a tall, emaciated creature with a face that was shiny like a mask. He wore a denim shirt tucked into his jeans and black, silver-toed boots. A thin, feminine chain swung at his hip to connect his wallet with an alligator clip at his belt. He resembled nothing so much as a wind-blown mummy reanimated and put in the clothes of a western cartoon character. We all stared at the dude as he sauntered down to the far pit, where he picked up two shoes with his long hands and rang them together once, softly, like a chime. He had gel in his hair, and he smelled like cologne.

The crowd circled in and got quiet.

Jorge walked up beside Terry and spoke to him out the side of his mouth. "You got any money left to lose?"

Terry leaned down and ground his tumbler into the grass. "You need to talk to my ex."

"You're the one should be suing her," Jorge said.

Terry made a humming sound of affirmation in the back of his throat. The two of them stood with their arms folded, squinting at their partners up at the far end of the yard. Terry sucked hard on the Newport.

"At least I've still got my beauty," Terry said. "She married me for my looks."

Jorge smiled. "What'd she leave you for?"

Terry cleared his throat and flicked the ash off the cigarette and bent down and picked his glass back up out of the grass.

Down at the far end, Mo pawed his white sneaker at the sand like a rhino. He tongued the dip in his bottom lip, spat, and told the dude beside him that he smelled like a whore.

"Let's go motherfucker!" Terry shouted. "Get your faggot ass in gear. I've got money to make."

The dude's face didn't do anything. He brought the horseshoe up even with his eyes, then he dropped his weight down low and slid forward on his left foot, swinging the shoe back and forward in a quick arc. The metal hissed out of his fingers, spun once and low in the air, and rung the pole. He stepped back and did the same thing with the other shoe.

"Motherfucker," said Terry.

"That's my man," whispered Jorge. Then he screamed it. Then Jorge pulled his white T-shirt up over his face and ran around in circles behind the pit. I passed the hat around again and bills started to pour in for Jorge and his dude. The silent stranger. The gunslinger. Fucking Clint Eastwood.

Jorge pulled the shirt off his head, and from where I stood, I could tell that his eyes weren't on the horseshoes or the dude or Terry but were instead focused intently on the hat as it made its way through the crowd of men—men in polo shirts tucked into checkered shorts with golf visors over their purple faces; men who had gone on to do little more in that time and place of plenty than to be consistently nothing other than themselves; men who had, following these brief and unchallenging and uncreative strictures, begun to amass wealth. They were big fish and had done nothing for it and knew it and didn't care, and this particular backwoods contest and all things like it functioned as their entertainment. Jorge watched them through narrowed eyes as they slipped bills out of their smooth leather wallets and flung them into the black hat with exaggerated, almost joyful, disdain.

Mo was still standing at the far end, poised, the heels of his sneakers touching like a big fat ballerina. He slid forward on his foot and he grunted and he let loose the shoe.

"We're going to beat you cocksuckers just like last week," Jorge whispered.

Mo's shoe spun way up, high and slow, and as it did, he held his pose there in the grass, back foot cocked out to the side, arm raised high as though summoning the desired result, and the whole place— I'm not exaggerating to say that the whole place, even the little kids—the whole place was just standing there silent, their eyes up in the air, watching the shoe turn and turn and turn.

The day after would've been a Sunday. In that case it must've been Monday when we saw the Qatari. I remember watching the crews roll in. I remember the excavators and the backhoe loaders. I remember the bulldozers on flatbeds, the skidders and the harvesters, and I remember the crew working fast to get the equipment off the trucks, eager to get after it. Terry walked downstairs and looked out the living room window and said that there was to be no work on this day.

He stood in his kitchen and drank his coffee until lunch and then he broke out the vodka. It got so noisy out in the woods that after a while I quit watching TV and stood at the picture window in the living room. It struck me that I'd never seen that many trees fall at once. The poor things looked surprised, like somebody had kicked them out of bed. Five, ten, fifteen. Boom boom boom, all day long.

After about half the bottle of vodka, Terry put on his Oakleys, and we both walked up through the woods. He was stiff-legged on bad knees as he stood at the edge of what he deemed to be the property line, then he took out his tape measure, and he started to make a lot of noise about *ten feet* and not an inch farther. About standard units goddamn it and none of this metric shit. The crew gave us a wide berth, peeking back every few minutes just to see that we weren't getting ourselves into trouble. It was after about the third or fourth peek that Terry unbuckled his pants, unzipped his fly, fished out his dick with a thumb and two fingers, and started to piss a shimmeringly clear and decently sized arc of urine onto the fresh dirt before him as he raised his middle finger high in the air.

It was five in the afternoon when a slick, red Jaguar pulled up into the field. From where I stood by the picture window, I could tell even before it stopped who was going to step out. He was in fact tall. He was in fact bony, and he did indeed have a head full of big black hair. I wouldn't have said *luxurious*, but I would bet that it took him some time with a hair dryer. He wore a loose sweater and linen pants, and after surveying the scene, he picked his way across the field in finely tooled loafers, hopping gingerly over the truck ruts. After a few yards of this, he stopped, bent down, and—very carefully, one-by-one—rolled up his pant cuffs.

The crew of workers all stopped what they were doing and flocked to him, jumped right out of the machines to gather before him, and when the Qatari was finished, he stood up, and he crossed his arms, and he nodded at the collective. They all began at once, waving and shouting and pointing their fingers at the picture window where we both now stood until finally the Qatari reached out over them with a long and quiet arm, as though he were conferring some sort of blessing. That arm hung there for a moment and then came down on the shoulder of one of the men, a young and stocky kid with a tight mustache, and with the laying of that hand, the crowd went silent. The men looked at their boots in the mud. They looked at the kid. They looked at the Qatari who held the kid's eyes for a beat in that silence, and then another. And then our man nodded. After he did so, the kid spoke to him, earnestly and with passion. Following the rhythm of the pauses in the kid's speech, the Qatari nodded along with him.

We waited until the meeting broke up and the men were back in their machines, and we watched the Qatari watching his men as they went about their obscure and diligent tasks all over that forest that they were slowly turning it into a red mud field. After a while the Qatari looked over to the house. He looked over for a long time, and we held that look as only one can when the divide between the observer and observed seems well nigh unbridgeable. Then he turned, and he walked back to his car.

We were out the back door like a shot, hustling over the grass, through the trees, across the mud ruts. We met that skinny sonofabitch on his side of the line, and we met him with ill intent.

"Hey." So here's Terry, coming up fast on stiff knees in his cargo shorts and sandals, pumping his arms, working hard not to break into a run.

"Hey." Terry in his Lyle Lovett T-shirt and his Budweiser ball cap and uncracked beercan jostling around in his hip pocket.

The earth-movers and dump trucks were bumping all around us, and the Qatari turned and saw us coming. And as he turned, he reached into his pocket and pulled out a pair of oil-black aviators and slipped them on. Then he put his hands on his hips.

"Hey." Terry pulled up short not two feet away. I stood a little behind and got a wide stance. I got right in that skinny bastard's periphery and just stared the cocksucker down.

"Listen up, Habib," Terry said to him. "You need to tell me who the fuck you think you are."

The Qatari smiled. Big even teeth. He looked at Terry, and then he turned and looked at me and the smile faded away. He looked up past us and he pursed his lips.

"You deaf, motherfucker?" That's what I said to him. I asked the motherfucker if he was deaf. I was hot. I moved over to one side to box him in, but he took a step back from the both of us, and then he turned his shoulders to face me.

"No, sir," he said. "I am not deaf." That's the way he talked.

"Look," Terry said, "I want to know what the fuck you think you're doing out here."

"Do you plan to assault me?" the Qatari said. "Should I be prepared to defend myself?" He put his hand in his pocket and pulled out a cellphone the size of a notebook. He looked at Terry as he tipped the phone at me, not even bothering to turn his head. "Do I need to contact the authorities?" He was taller up close, the Qatari. And he was looking down at Terry, and he was done smiling.

"Go ahead," Terry said. "I'll tell you the sheriff's number."

The Qatari kept bobbing the phone at me and

then turned his hand and bobbed it at Terry, as if the phone were going to say the words he wasn't. Finally, he slipped it back in his pocket. He put his hands on his hips and nodded his head out to the strip of trees, to the outline of the house behind it.

"That is your house," he said.

"That's right," said Terry.

"It is a lovely house."

"Don't talk about my house to me."

"It is a lovely house, and one that you are lucky to have."

"You're lucky I haven't stomped your skinny ass flat into this field."

"Beautiful wooden beams," the Qatari said. "All old growth. A magnificent fireplace."

"What do you know about it?"

The guy gave Terry a tight little smile. He looked at the dirt and then looked away for a second, and then he sighed, like his mind had wandered away from us entirely. Then he turned back.

He said—very quietly he said—"That house belongs to a woman."

I looked at Terry. Terry didn't say shit.

"Blond woman," the guy went on, faster now. "Quite lovely. She is often at the Lightfoot Grille. Is that the name of it? I can't remember. You see, I'm not from here." That big smile again. "She enjoys the salmon," he said, "and the Chardonnay. She'd never had a true Chablis, but she appreciated it very much that I found one for her on the menu." He paused, that smile filling up the silence. "In any event," he finally said, "it is a charming house. And regardless of whomever I would call here, he would most likely ask you to leave my property, and not the other way round."

He stood there and he waited for us to say something. He could have waited all day.

"Allow me to imagine something," the Qatari said.

"Fuck you," said Terry.

"Allow me to imagine this. Allow me to imagine that it was good for you to have a house in this place. That you found it peaceful. That your life may be otherwise unsteady but that here you feel safe."

"Fuck you."

"You came here,"—the guy didn't even pause—"you came here when? It doesn't matter. You came here, and you found this place. And now you have come to me because you want to know what it is that I plan to do."

Terry spit in the dirt.

"Very well," the guy said. He waved around his hand. "I plan to scrape all of this." Those were his words. Scrape. "Down to the rock," he said. "I plan to remove those hills. Cut it all back. Who can say what will happen then? Some single-family homes?" he said. Then he shrugged. "Perhaps a Blockbuster."

"Motherfucker," Terry said, and he didn't move. He didn't lift his hand or take a step and he said "motherfucker" one more time, like he was talking to himself.

The Qatari was smiling again, looking from one

of us to the other as though testing to see if a joke had properly landed, but then his smile faded again—he couldn't quite seem to hold it—and he nodded at us, short and hard, just like he had nodded at the kid with the mustache.

"Who do you think I am?" he finally said. "Or perhaps you don't. Perhaps this would give me nothing." He lowered his head and he took off those aviators and held them down at his waist. He polished the lenses with the edge of his sweater, and he slid them back on. "Forgive me," he said. "I have been known to speak out of turn. My wife," he said. "When I am feeling poorly, this is what she says. She says, *My love*. This is what she calls me. She says, *My love, look to the sky. The sky outlives everything. Even suffering.*"

Then he tilted his chin up at the clouds for us, as if to demonstrate. It was one of those gray summer days kicked up by the river, hot and flat and pale all the way down to the pitch black trees.

"She got that out of a book," he said.

Then he turned and walked back to the Jaguar. Terry stood there in the open field and watched him go, watched his skinny ass pick all the way back across the mud ruts. Once the guy got to the car, he turned back around. I realized then that he was the kind who couldn't help himself.

The Qatari opened the door, and he lifted up his chin and shouted to us over the noise of all of the trucks. What he said was, "Is it not true, my friend, that there are things much bigger than the sky?"

It was about two years after that when I finally saw Cynthia again. I was home for the summer, and it had become a regular thing for my sister and I to get frozen yogurt after lunch. The Pinkberry out past Purcellville was the only such place for twenty miles, and would remain so for at least another year, so she and I would drive out to Round Hill and wait the requisite ten minutes so the tired flagman could let the pavers on Route 7 Business finish their most recent pass on the extra lanes that were being added to what had been for close to fifty years a rough and sleepy stretch headed nowhere west.

After the sort of wait that makes you anxious and bitter and cruel, my sister and I would pull into the strip mall that lay across Terry's property like a T-square pointing hard northeast. Or rather Cynthia's property. Or Cynthia's old property. We were sitting out under the awning next to the Subway a few doors down from the Giant, and I had been looking out at the parking lot, at the sea of cars that shook in the sun and at the field beyond that lot, at the naked dirt where the fresh asphalt crusted off in little black crumbs. Beyond that dirt lay the treeline, jagged and stripped and freshly exposed—just a hint of green in the low scrub, the young warped trees at the edge of it pale and leafless like worms.

And so as all of this was percolating in my head, I wasn't completely shocked to feel a light but insistent touch on my shoulder, and I turned to see no one other than Cynthia standing at my side, grande Starbucks in her manicured hands.

"Hey," she said to me.

"Hey," I said. I sat there and watched her watch me as she tapped one hard pink nail on the back of her brown hand. "Cynthia," I said after a moment, "this is my sister, Charlotte."

"Hey," Charlotte said, squinting as she looked up.

"How are things?" Cynthia said to me.

"Good," I said. "Back at school."

"I thought so," she said. "Good for you."

"How about you?"

"I'm down in Pentagon City," she said. "So I'm not out here too often, either."

I looked out at the parking lot, and I thought about the easy thing to say. I looked back and saw that her face was braced for that very thing. I didn't say it. "Pentagon City's nice," I said.

"Look," she said. Then she didn't say anything else. I let her stand there, tapping her fingernail on her hand like the seconds of a clock. Tick tick tick. She looked out at the parking lot, and then looked back.

"You seen Terry?" I asked.

Her face broke into a smile and then closed back up. "It's not," she started. Then she smiled again. "Have you?"

I told her I hadn't. I told her I had no idea what happened to him. I said he could be anywhere at this point. Back up with his family in Michigan. Down in Florida getting sauced on the beach. Or maybe he'd moved out to the Arabian Peninsula and bought up some real estate. "How expensive," I asked, "could

UP FROM GRUNDY

"You," Coach said, "are a loser. Feel that for a second. I bet it hurts something awful."

Coach sat on the orange bedspread with his chapped fingers folded up tight in front of him. Coach with his mustache. Coach who smelled like Skoal and sweat in his polo shirt and too-tight khakis that he had to pinch at the thighs so he could sit down right. The mattress creaked underneath him, and from where Byron sat in the motel room chair, the bulge of Coach's crotch was all he could see.

Byron turned his head away from the man before him and looked around the room at the worn-out carpets and limp curtains and the drop ceiling. It wasn't late, but it was dark, and outside the roads were covered with ice and sand and salt that would still be there when the next storm came down from Tennessee.

"You showed some guts to get here," Coach said. "*Guts*," he said again, and his face crinkled up like a

Qatar be, compared to what we're looking at here?"

I thought that was funny. A little funny, so I smiled, pleased with myself, but Cynthia wasn't smiling. She looked as though I'd made a joke about the dead.

"It's *cutter*," she said.

"What is?"

"How you say it. The country." She kept looking at me, her face pulled tight as a drum. And then she said, "Okay." She looked back out at the parking lot and said, "Well, it was nice to see you," and she walked off the curb and up the aisle of cars. I watched her go, moving quickly in her linen pants and her sleeveless blouse, her gold earrings knocking against the sides of her neck.

"Who was that?" my sister asked around her spoonful of yogurt.

"Old friend," I said, as I watched Cynthia's small black Mercedes pull out of the aisles and take the right out to 7. And as it paused for a few seconds with the blinker flashing, I thought I could see someone in the passenger seat. I am probably making this up—a willed illusion perpetrated on my too young and eager and overactive brain. But I could've sworn I saw a big man in a crumpled ballcap, hunched forward, uncomfortable, too big for the car.

"You don't know anybody like that," my sister said, chewing on her spoon.

bag. "All right, now look here," he said. "That boy tonight wasn't any better than you. Wasn't any faster. Any stronger. I tell you what that boy tonight was."

"What was he, Coach?" Byron said, his eyes still on the ceiling.

Coach's hands gripped each other. "Son," he said. "You listen to what I'm trying to tell you. You worked your tail off to get out here. You flew through districts and nobody saw you coming and at regionals? Nobody had you over that boy from Stonewall. What was his name? That boy's name?"

"Barlow."

"Barlow." Coach nodded. "Big son of a bitch. Nobody had you over him. Nobody said, 'Hey, son, you're gonna wreck this boy's train.' Nobody said that. Nobody but one body. And who was that body?" Byron looked at his hands, so Coach raised his chin and said it again, "Who was that body?"

"You," said Byron.

"Damn right," said Coach. He stood up off the bed and sat back down, and he pulled on the sleeve of his jacket. "I'll tell you why right now," Coach said. "It's because I could see something in you from the word go, son. And you went out there that night and you wrecked that boy's train. You wrecked it good."

The more Coach talked, the wider his eyes became until the whole scene of the regional tournament could be playing across the backs of them. He jerked his shoulders.

"*Boom*!" Coach said, popping his elbow into his open hand. "Hard crossface! Up and over," he shouted, and Coach was up off the bed again, swimming in the air with his arms to imitate the moves as he ticked them off. "Wrist control, get the half in, get it in deep, walk it over. Walk it all the way over and *pinned*," he shouted. "Barlow's on his back!"

Byron had heard it before and he didn't want to hear it now, but Coach wanted to hear it because Coach knew he was right. Nobody had Byron winning the district at the beginning of the season, and nobody went out to regionals to watch him beat up the Barlow kid—nobody except Coach, who had driven Byron down to Grundy for the state wrestling tournament in his own pickup and paid for these hotel rooms out of his pocket because Coach knew what it was.

Coach was the only one who knew what it was, and now Coach leaned over in the motel room and he put his elbows on his knees. He was older up close. He dyed his hair. His cheeks were littered with broken blood vessels. Byron shifted in his chair.

"Now that boy tonight," said Coach. "That boy was scared. Not scared of you. Local boy. Grew up out here. Coal miners, son, I know it. They're my people. And that boy knew everybody in that whole damn room. Knew the music they played over the P.A. Knew the mat you both got down on with your hands and your knees. Did you even get a good look at him? You see his people up in those stands? That boy ain't going to college. He ain't got no desk job waiting for him. You were going in there for a—look at me—you were going in there for a coronation. You thought you deserved it. And that boy over there knew something else. He felt the breath of the beast, son. Listen to me now."

In between lecturing on how aliens brought civilization to Earth from Alpha Centauri and leaning out the door to leer at the soccer girls that passed by in the hallways, Coach taught algebra. He taught it in a dress shirt that he kept shoving back down into his pants, his chest high and his hair in all directions. "Math," he'd say, "is like wrestling. Wrestling is like time. Time is like God. God is like Math. And wrestling is nothing other than the sport of God. With whom—tell me, boy—with whom does Jacob wrestle for a night and a day? The scholars will tell you that it is an angel, but the scholars have not read. No, sir. They eschew the original text. Didn't think I knew that word, did you? And what cannot be eschewed must be embraced. That's Shakespeare, son. And they say I'm the math teacher. *Merry Wives*. I wouldn't know much about that, though. Never been to Windsor, neither. All right, now, who can tell me about Brahmagupta?"

He'd settled on Byron early. He saw a long kid with a thick neck who hadn't even thought about wrestling. Coach talked him into the first practice easily because Byron was easily talked into things. Coach could see that, too, and knew that it would have to be burned out of him, so on the very first day, Coach ran Byron with the varsity. He ran him up and down the hallways that smelled like bleach until

Byron puked into a trashcan, and then Coach ran him some more.

Coach ran him, and he said, in front of the whole team he said, "You thought you had this all figured out, didn't you, boy?" He said, "You think you've had it tough? You don't know what tough is. You don't know what real work is. What it is to see a man across from you face-to-face. What it is to know there ain't no other way out but through him."

Byron ran harder. Ran with bile in his cheeks. And he ran not to beat the kid next to him, even though he did that each time down and back (did it easy, not even a contest), no—Byron ran to show that smug motherfucker with the whistle in his teeth that he didn't give a shit who he was. Line 'em up. I'll bury every single one of your boys. Your boys and you, too, if you want to keep flapping your mouth.

Coach watched it all for a while. He liked the kid's speed. He liked his easy turns at the far end of the hallway, and he especially liked the way the kid would eyeball him every time down and back. After a while Coach blew the whistle. He sent the boys back to the mats, and he pulled Byron aside.

Coach sat the boy down. He got him a paper cup of orange Gatorade, and he took a seat next to him but didn't put his arm around him because he knew it was too soon to touch him. After the boy finished, Coach stood and said, "Follow me," and they both walked back down the hallway to the trophy case by the gym doors, a small and dusty hutch. The glass front was dim with cleaner that never got rubbed all the way out and they both stood before it and Coach didn't say anything for a few minutes. Then, he leaned down and pointed out, in the back behind the footballs, the grainy picture of the last state wrestling champ, 1972. A skinny kid with big hair on the top step, holding a small plaque at his waist. That's when Coach said, "Look at this." Coach said, "I don't show this to kids. No reason to." He said, "I'm showing this to you. Look at him. This boy in the middle of all this. This boy's still here," Coach said. "He's here, and he's not going anywhere. It's like he never left. Like he never got old. Never got slow. And he'll still be here when you do. This boy's up here forever."

Coach stayed where he was, with his eyes on the back of the case and his hands on his knees. And Byron couldn't tell if Coach was doing it for him, stretching this out into something rehearsed, or if he was still down there in that picture for another reason unguessed. After a while Coach turned around and looked back up the empty hall. He said, "You tell me what gets to be there."

Coach was getting hot in the motel room.

"It's not that you get to be the champ," Coach said. "It's that the champ gets to be you." He was up in a low crouch, slapping the back of his hand into his palm. "Pow! And that boy's the champ," Coach said, swinging his outstretched finger to the closed shades. "He's the champ and you ain't, and you'll never be because you got too much to care about."

"Coach," said Byron. "I'm done."

Coach froze.

"I'm done," said Byron.

Coach looked at the boy where he sat, slumped in his sweatpants with his hoodie up over his head and his white-sock feet. Coach closed his mouth, and he stood all the way up. He pulled at the edge of his jacket. Pulled on it twice. His fingers moved to the buttons, and he snapped closed a few of them, and then he turned without a word and walked across the room to the door and he yanked it open and walked out into the night and the door hissed closed behind him.

Byron let out his breath. He looked back up at the drop ceiling, and he looked over at the bathroom. He thought about showering, but he didn't get up. He took a few deep breaths, and as he did so, he felt his chest rise and fall against his T-shirt. He could feel every muscle of his body. He could feel them running long and loose down his arms and down the backs of his legs until they slipped into the bones of his hands and his feet. He was in the best shape of his life and he knew it and he knew there was nothing he could do about it. He looked at the phone. He looked at the shower.

The door opened again and the cold air ran back into the room. Coach was standing on the sidewalk, his hand flat against the door. He had on a big brown Carhartt jacket, his gut high and tight against a white T-shirt. He was standing there against the night in that bad light of motel rooms. Green and sick. Coach said, "Get up. Get your shoes on. We ain't done."

The first time Byron saw the fireman's throw it looked too obvious, too simple. He saw two wrestlers in the video, head-to-head, grinding and pulling at one another until one pushed the other back up on his heels. The man getting pushed reached out for a wrist, crouched down on the mat, and then used the other's momentum to slip underneath him. He jammed his arm up to the elbow between the man's open legs and then flipped him onto his back for the pin. It looked like the most natural thing in the world.

The first time Byron tried the fireman's in practice he got caught kneeling on the mat with his arms up over his head. His partner spun behind him, grabbed Byron's arms, leveraged his elbow right between Byron's shoulders, and pushed his head over his knees and down into the mat. He held Byron there for over a minute, dragging him around on his face until his teeth cut open his lips.

When Byron asked Coach to show him the fireman's, Coach made him practice it for thirty minutes straight. "You see the long hand on that clock, don't you? I'm asking you a question. That long hand, son, is the one you'll want to be following. From the six to the twelve. You track that thing across half of that big white clock face. Track that thing like a bird, like a big black bird across the face of the moon, and the owl of Minerva only flies at midnight. You tell me what that means, and I'll let you knock off early."

Byron never did figure out what that meant, and thirty straight minutes of a three-second move left Byron shaking. But he got it. The wrist, the drop, the loop, the flip, every piece coming together until it was all one thing. After a week Byron could do it with his eyes closed, and half the time he did. Coach made Byron practice it on the mats and out in the hallways. Coach made him practice it with a tackling dummy he snuck out of the football equipment room and he made him practice it on a string of kids all lined up and waiting for it. As Byron got better, he added a little something special at the end. What Byron did was, he stood up.

He stood up with the man draped across his back like a sack of potatoes, and then he'd rise on one foot. Up on his toes—this is the part that would take forever, like the two seconds at the top of a rollercoaster. Look around, son, you can see the whole park. And the first time Byron twisted his shoulder around and dropped all of it right down in the middle of his partner's chest, it made the kind of sound that made people look away. Coach didn't look away.

"Hot *damn!*" is what Coach said.

Byron got called on it every once in a while. He lost a few matches while kids were lying on the mat, croaking like frogs. But Byron won enough to get to districts, to get to regionals, to get to states. Coach started to shout out in practice that Byron was going to murder every sonofabitch in the country under 175 and there wasn't anything anybody could do about it, and Byron heard it and he believed it. And all the while the fireman's throw got so deep in him that it felt easier than saying his own name. He flipped that move over in his sleep and he did it perfect every time, like a key in a lock. Byron could even feel himself do it in the motel room chair, and when Coach opened up the door, Byron knew he had to get up and stop feeling that move he was never going to be able to pull again without going to jail.

"You think you're too good for it," Coach said.

He turned the steering wheel and shook his head out at the dark road and the headlights that scanned it. They drove through a stop sign and down into a holler and back out again. The trees hung close to the road.

"Always did," Coach said. "You didn't even want to wrestle. Never even liked it. Not that I could tell what it was that you did like. Go out and get in trouble with all the rest of the delinquents, I suppose. What do you think they're doing out there right now? Running with bad company and burning up time, but all right, then, here's what I'm saying."

"What are you saying."

"Goddamn it, what I'm saying is that if you think this is about wrestling, then you've got it wrong, son. Flat wrong. You're looking past the wrestling," Coach said. "Fine. Not everybody needs it. But here's what it says. It says—I'm talking about wrestling here—it says that you've got to give that other man over there his dignity. Got to recognize that he's just as much a man as you, and he thinks he deserves it, too. And that's why you've got to crush him. Without mercy. If you cheat him he'll know it and he won't forgive it and it shouldn't be forgiven."

They came out into a wide dark valley. Green eyes popped out in the fields and closed back into the dark.

Coach looked over to the boy just long enough so the boy knew he was looking and then he turned back. And Coach held that silence because he wanted the next line to stick with the boy but when he went to speak his voice failed him altogether, and the line came out in a whisper. The second Coach heard it, he wished he hadn't. Wished he had said it a different way. Thought, 'Well, now it's said and what can we do with that. What can we do with what's out there. A goddamn whisper like some damned dead and gone ghost.'

They took a turn and rode up high on a ridge and back down onto a pale gravel road. Through the dark Byron could see the lights of a house hanging against the black, the trees rushing by, unimportant.

The kitchen counter was scattered with newspapers, bills, coupon inserts, empty potato chip bags and half-eaten loaves of coffee cake. She was somewhere past forty, with frosted bangs and a big chin. Heavy hands and thick shoulders and calves. The skin was peeling around her green eyes.

"You should've told me you were coming, Chip," she said to Coach. "You should've told me you were coming and that you had company." She looked down the counter at the plastic bags of food. "I could've fixed something," she said. She dropped her hand on the counter. "I can get you some tea," she said. "Do you like tea?"

"Thank you, Deidre, I'll have some tea and so will this young man," Coach said. "Deidre, this is Byron. We were at the wrestling tournament today, and Byron here took second."

"Did he."

"That's a fact."

"You're good, are you?"

"I took second."

"It's not first."

"No ma'am."

"So, who's better than you?"

"Boy from Grundy."

"Well, there's no arguing with that," she said, and as she said it, a long and a mournful groan came from further back in the house. The sound of a man calling in his sleep.

Byron looked from Coach to his sister, and neither behaved as though they'd heard anything at all. Coach stood straight-backed, a big empty smile on his face.

"I've brought Byron here because I want him to meet Greg," Coach said.

Deidre nodded her head once, hard. Her jaw was set. "Okay," she said.

"I want Byron to meet Greg, and I want to talk about Greg's history and about his sacrifice."

The empty moan came again.

"Okay," said Deidre, and she closed her eyes and nodded again.

"Greg," Coach said, "is a hero. The kind of hero of which we are in short supply. Isn't that right,

Deidre?"

Deidre turned around to the stove. She kept her back to them and busied her hands with the water and the pot and the little box of tea bags. "Greg is a hero," she said.

"That's right," said Coach. "Greg is a hero and a man to be admired for what he's done, and to be understood as a model for what he's given."

Deidre turned back from the stove and she looked at Coach. She put her hands on the countertop and she pushed her chin forward as though she were about to say what had been said before and needn't be said again. Her eyes were on her brother, and Coach's face was tight and pleading. Deidre turned back to the stove.

"Let's go say hello to Greg," she said, and she walked into the den.

The man sat crank-sided in the chair. His head listed back, the bones of his face twisted up as though stretched and left to dry. His Velcro shoes sat sideways on the footrest, and his bad arm lay tight against his ribs, the curled fist up near his chin. It gave Byron the eerie impression that the man was lost in thought.

"Hello, sir," said Coach, and he bent forward at the waist. "It's been a while, hasn't it? Been a while, indeed."

"Six months," said Deidre, and she took a seat in a deep chair by the doorway.

"Six months," said Coach. "Well." He patted his

hand against his own leg.

The man in the chair sat silent. A thick black strap held his glasses on his face, and it was difficult for Byron to see his eyes.

"Well, sir, I've come by with a friend of mine, and I want to introduce him to you. I wanted him to meet you. Greg, this is Byron."

Coach opened his hand by his side, indicating where he wanted Byron to stand. Byron walked up and stood there and looked down at the man gaping in the chair.

"Greg is an Iraqi War veteran," said Coach. "First sergeant, U.S. Army. Isn't that right, sir?"

The man in the chair remained as he was.

"Go on there, son. Shake his hand."

"I won't."

"What do you mean you won't?"

"I mean, I don't want to shake his hand. I don't want to shake his hand."

"He ain't going to hurt you, boy. You go over there and take that man's hand and you give it a shake and you thank him for his service."

Byron didn't move.

"You won't touch him and you see what he's done for you?" Coach's voice was even and quiet. All the edge to it was gone. He said, "You won't even pay him the common decency of shaking his hand?"

Byron bit the inside of his cheek. He looked at the floor and he took a step. And then another. As he came closer to the chair, he could see the man's gray and watery eyes where they took in the ceiling. Byron leaned over and picked up the free hand that sat in a limp fist by the man's thigh. It was cool to the touch and damp, the skin loose around the bones. Byron could only think of handling a dead chicken.

"First Sergeant Greg served two tours in Mosul," said Coach. "Two tours in which he was highly decorated." Coach moved to the couch and took a seat, and Byron sat beside him. Coach continued to speak, and he did so as though he were addressing a large group of people in the otherwise empty room. He spoke about Greg's deployment and of his time in the desert, and Byron noticed that Deidre had begun to nod at the rhythm of what he said. Coach continued to explain that Greg had been a leader to those who were under his command, and that he'd demonstrated what it meant to be a model for American men everywhere.

"What happened to him?" Byron said.

The man in the wheelchair whipped his head to the side. The headrest rattled, and then he was still.

Coach's smile stayed where it was. He looked at Byron and said, "Well, son, he's right there. Why don't you ask him? Don't speak about him like he ain't right here. He's right here, ain't he, Deidre?"

Deidre stood and she walked into the kitchen.

Byron said, "What happened to you, sir?"

"What do you mean what happened," said Coach.

"I mean." Byron stopped. "I mean, how did he get into the wheelchair."

"It was a roadside bomb, wasn't it, Greg?"

Greg didn't move.

"It was a roadside bomb," said Coach. "Twenty klicks outside of Mosul, and his team rolled up on a—"

"It was thirty klicks, Chip," said Deidre. She walked back in with three steaming mugs on a plastic tray. She handed a mug to Coach and to Byron and then returned to her chair. "It was thirty klicks," she said. "And you always get this part wrong. It was thirty klicks, and you're going to say it was a camel, but it wasn't a camel."

Greg twisted hard in the chair. He slammed his free arm against the armrest and moaned.

"It wasn't a camel," Deidre said loudly. "It was an ox. And I don't know where they got an ox from but they had an ox and—"

"And they'd wired that ox up every which way," said Coach. "Tricked it up something awful, didn't they, Greg?" Coach held this question open, and they all three sat watching the man in the chair relax by patient degrees into stillness.

Byron looked from brother to sister.

"Something awful," Coach said. "And you didn't have to get but so close to that thing, and look out."

"Look out," repeated Deidre quietly. Her eyes were on Greg, and she sipped her tea from her mug that she held in both hands, and she looked over to the man in the chair as though he were not what he was but was instead a full and hale and healthy man.

From somewhere upstairs, Byron could hear the ticking of a clock. Greg moaned once, and he began to rock, the chair swinging gently beneath him.

"Easy there, Greg," Diedre said, and she said it like she were speaking to a horse.

The man slowed and stopped.

"They're getting you all worn out, aren't they," Deidre said. She shook her head. "You two," she said, and there was teasing in her voice, as though Greg had been taken out for a hard night of strippers and booze. She said, "You two have come over and just worn him slam out." Deidre took another sip of her tea. Then she cleared her throat and sat up. "Jerry's supposed to come over later to help me, but you two have worn him out early," she said. "Look at him. His head's drooping on his chest. His head's drooping on his chest and he's got to get some sleep. Chip, get Greg up to bed for us."

"You need me to pick him up?"

"Pick him up and take him up the stairs for us."

Greg's free hand flew to his face.

"I need you to get him into bed," Deidre said. "And once you get him there, I'll put him down. That's right, Greg, Chip's going to get you to bed and I'll put you down. Look at him. It's time for him to go to bed. You're tired, aren't you, honey. These two boys have worn you slam out."

Greg had begun to moan again. The sound was hollow and wobbly, and it rose up high and then choked on itself. Then it started again.

"He's beat, Chip," Deidre said loudly. "Help me get him up."

Coach looked over to Byron. "I think the boy should do it," he said.

Deidre was standing slowly in the noise and she brushed at her robe and she said, "Chip, quit the bull-shit now and help me out."

"I ain't doing it," said Coach, and his eyes were wide and serious on Byron.

"I'm not," said Byron.

"Chip, come on now."

Greg had begun to rock in his chair. His moaning found a single pitch and held it.

"The boy is going to learn what it is to give a United States veteran a hand and to help him to end his day."

"Chip, I don't need help getting him into bed. I need to get him up the stairs and we can't wait for Jerry."

Greg's head slapped back and forth against the headrest, and his glasses were getting turned around on his face.

"I said we're getting you there, honey."

Byron shouted over the noise, "Don't you have one of those things?"

"What things?"

"One of those things." He waved his hand at the staircase. "Those things on the stairs."

"What the hell are you talking about?"

"Those things—the elevator, staircase things. Conveyor belt. Ah, shit."

"Escalators?"

"Yeah, like an escalator."

"Like at the mall? Who the hell is this kid? Son, what is wrong with you. Escalator."

"I mean, a rail. A fucking rail like you see on TV!"

"A rail?"

"Yeah, a rail! Into the wall."

"Do you know how much those things cost?"

Byron raised his hands.

"Of course you don't," shouted Coach. "Of course you don't know. You don't know because you can walk up and down the goddamn stairs on your own two legs."

Byron stood with his eyes closed and said, "I'll do it. I'll just do it."

After Greg had calmed down, Byron walked up to him in the chair. He reached back and peeled off the straps around Greg's chest and his lap. The body rocked in the chair like driftwood, and as Byron leaned in, he could smell feces and milk. Greg's eyes remained on the ceiling, and Byron reached for Greg's good hand. He took the man's wrist between his fingers and then Byron bent down, his head low to the ground like he were searching for something in the carpet. He eased into Greg and he drew Greg's arm across his own shoulders and then he rocked away, drawing the man out of the chair and onto Byron's back, and then Byron slipped his free arm around the twisted and frozen legs. As Byron stood, Greg drooled a long white string of spit down onto the floor.

Coach followed them across the room and he followed them up the stairs. At the top of the hall, Coach walked ahead and turned into a room at the end and clicked on the light. Byron walked down the hall with the hollow body on his back, past the dim pictures that hung there, and Byron didn't turn to see who was in them. As he came into the brightness of the room, he bent back down to his knee. He slowly rolled the muscles in his shoulders and rose and pulled his arm back out from around the legs, and he lay the long, limp arm down beside Greg on the fully-made bed.

Byron stood up and looked around. Coach was standing by the footboard. His hands were at his sides.

"He was a good man," Coach said. His eyes were on Greg where he lay silent on the bedspread. "They wanted kids. Had a good job out at the Wellmore mine." Coach stopped. He cleared his throat. "He had achieved nothing of note," Coach said.

Deidre came into the room and she walked past Byron. As she walked to the foot of the bed, Coach stepped back. Deidre reached down and took up one of Greg's feet and she peeled off the Velcro straps of Greg's oversized shoes.

"You think he's less than a man, and I'm going to tell you he's more," Coach said. "He's something for us to, to look upon. To ponder. His body. Byron, do you see what I'm trying to say?"

Byron turned and he saw Coach standing next to him. Standing close enough to touch. But Byron didn't touch him, and Coach kept looking at the man on the bed as Deidre flipped the shoes off onto the floor. One, and then the other. And then Coach asked the question again.

JAPANESE MAPLES

When we first came to look at the house, the owner sat out on the back deck pretending to be deaf. My pregnant wife and I kept calling out hello as the owner stared up at the trees with sunglasses on her face. I didn't think much of it at the time—I was more worried about the state of the place: the remedial kitchen, the tangled and overgrown basement—but I've heard since that the old bat kept up the deaf act for several buyers who'd been by previously. It's unclear why she did it, but it might've had something to do with her flat refusal to leave the house, even after signing the contract. She'd been alone in the place for decades, a retired documentary filmmaker. Stills from her work hung down the hallways.

After we moved in, our neighbors told us that a few years earlier, she had decided to cut down a whole flock of Japanese maples that had rung the property. These things are, if you're not familiar, both expensive and gorgeous: low-domed trees with delicate leaves of a color purple you don't often find outside the skin of a plum. I used to stand on the porch after dinner, looking at the yard and wondering where they had been, why she did it. Had they gotten too big? Were they diseased? Had she just lost the wherewithal to keep them up, given the demands of everything else?

But one evening as we sat outside, watching our one-year-old stand and stagger and fall in the grass, our next-door neighbor—another old and solitary woman—confided that the owner had told her that the purple trees were evil, were suspicious growths installed and given succor by a satanic power. The old woman had gone on to tell our neighbor that she was being repeatedly raped by the boy with cerebral palsy who lived across the street in a white-porticoed house, and that every home on the block that featured a white portico was a reservoir of evil influence, a portal for energies malicious and untoward. In fact, so our neighbor told us, the filmmaker would shuffle around the neighborhood at dusk, pocket notebook in hand, taking notes on all such properties that tended toward darkness, that possessed something unspeakable, something irrational and fleeting and impermanently contained.

ABOUT
THE AUTHOR

Cameron MacKenzie's work has appeared in *Salmagundi*, *The Michigan Quarterly Review*, *The Rumpus*, and *CutBank*, among other places. His novel, *The Beginning of His Excellent and Eventful Career*, was called "poignant, brutal, and beautiful" by *Kirkus Reviews*, and "visionary" by *Rain Taxi*. *River Weather* is his first collection of short stories. He lives in Roanoke, Virginia.

ACKNOWLEDGMENTS

This book would have been impossible without the inexhaustible optimism, encouragement, and insight of Tim Fitts, as well as that of John Wall Barger, Mary Crockett Hill, Susan Barr-Toman, R. H. Schmitt, Robert Boyers, Adam Berlin, Jeffery Heiman, Kathleen Volk Miller, and so many others who have given these stories their valuable time and consideration.

"Kalim Mansour" appeared in *Salmagundi*.

"Coyotes" appeared in *CutBank*.

"A Non-Smoking House" appeared in *J Journal*.

"Rowdy" appeared in *Painted Bride Quarterly*, and was nominated for the 2020 Pushcart Prize.

"Up from Grundy" appeared in *Able Muse*, and was nominated for the 2018 Pushcart Prize.

COLOPHON

The edition you are holding is the First Edition of this publication.

The title is set in Manolete, created by Woodcutter. The sans serif font is set in Avenir Book, created by Adrian Frutiger. The Alternating Current Press logo is set in Portmanteau, created by JLH Fonts. All other text is set in Iowan Old Style, created by John Downer. All fonts used with permission; all rights reserved.

Cover artwork designed by Leah Angstman, with image by Andre Ludi. The Alternating Current lightbulb logo created by Leah Angstman, ©2013, 2021 Alternating Current. All images used with permission; all rights reserved.

Other Works from
ALTERNATING CURRENT PRESS

All of these books (and more) are available at
Alternating Current's website: press.alternatingcurrentarts.com.

alternatingcurrentarts.com

Made in United States
North Haven, CT
18 December 2021